WIZARD

HOUNDS OF HELLFIRE MC

FIONA DAVENPORT

Copyright © 2025 by Fiona Davenport

Cover designed by Elle Christensen

Edited by Jenny Sims (Editing4Indies)

All rights reserved.

No part of this book may be reproduced in any form or by any electronic or mechanical means, including information storage and retrieval systems, without written permission from the author, except for the use of brief quotations in a book review.

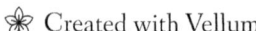 Created with Vellum

WIZARD

Baylor "Wizard" Chadwick didn't think he'd fall hard and fast for a woman like a few of his club brothers had recently done. Not until the Hounds of Hellfire tech expert saw Thea Drummond's photo during a background check.

Thea didn't trust Wizard's motive when the biker asked her out. Too many guys assumed awful things about her because she was a steamy romance author. Wizard worked on breaking down her walls, but just as they started to grow close, someone else tried to stake their claim on Thea.

PROLOGUE
WIZARD

I ended the call with my club brother and scanned the notes I'd taken during our conversation. Echo was on active surveillance for a ring of con men that the Hounds of Hellfire, my motorcycle club, was trying to take down. Apparently, the female neighbor had perfect access—at least, that was the story he was spinning—and he wanted me to do a background check. Possibly a deep dive if anything looked questionable.

Since I had several programs that basically ran on their own, they were searching for specific information about the thieves, which left me free to work on Echo's request. Even though most of the background check was done by the computer, I always went through everything. When all was said and done, I would never believe that a robot was better than the human eye. Even if I designed it.

Violet Kimball. Twenty years old. Single. Audiobook narrator.

An audiobook narrator? That job could be a cover for many things, but that didn't mean I would find anything else.

I pulled up her list of credits and noticed she'd done the majority of her work for a romance author, Thea Drummond. It was a beautiful name, and I wondered if it was real or a pen name. Curiosity got the best of me, so I started digging into Thea.

Despite the fact that I was supposed to be looking into Violet, I let the program run on her and focused on Thea. I was shocked when I looked at her address and realized she only lived about twenty minutes away in the next town over. I could have run into her and never even known it. But then, as a tech genius, I spent most of my time behind a screen...so maybe not.

She was twenty-two. Single. Never married. Went to a college a few hours from Riverstone, Georgia—the town where my MC was located—but dropped out between her junior and senior year when her independently published books began to make her enough money to write full-time.

Parents moved to Arizona when she was eighteen. She had an older sister, Cady. They didn't appear to have a strong relationship since Thea's phone records indicated they only spoke once or twice a year. And her travel had never taken her to Michigan, where Cady lived.

I continued to build a picture of her life story through all the facts I was compiling until I got a text, pulling me out of the little bubble I'd built around myself. After answering the message, I remembered Echo's request and figured I should look into Violet before I got lost in Thea again.

While compiling her dossier, I pulled up one of her audiobooks and hit play.

Before long, I was sucked into the story. Until she reached a steamy scene, and the thought of listening to the Echo's girl pretending to have sex made me flinch.

But I was too hooked on the story to stop reading, so I purchased the e-book on my computer and quickly found my spot.

Holy fuck.

After the first couple of paragraphs, I went back to the information I'd been gathering and found a picture of her. My lungs froze, and my body stirred when her face appeared on my screen.

Light blond hair hung in silky waves around her shoulders. Her forest-green eyes were fringed by dark lashes. She had an oval-shaped face with high cheekbones, a button nose, and full lips. Fucking gorgeous.

Her last report from her doctor said she was an average weight for her size. I couldn't help noticing that some of that came from her generous tits. I glanced at her height and chuckled. She was only five foot two. At six foot four, I would tower over her, but I liked that it would make her so petite next to me. She would fit perfectly into the grooves of my body, and I could just carry her around. Or if she was being stubborn, I'd simply pick her up and put her where I wanted her to be.

With her picture in my head, I went back to reading. When the scene was done, I was sweating, and my pants were so tight it was almost painful. The couple on the pages had become Thea and me, making me ache to run my hands all over her body, kiss those pink lips, and feel her pussy squeezing my cock.

I set the e-reader down and thought about anything that would cool my libido, then I tried to get back to work. However, my mind kept wandering back to the story, and not the sex—well...not *only* the sexy part. I was curious about the suspense, wondering how she would resolve the conflict with the villain and between the main couple. After a half hour of staring at my computer and getting nothing done, I told myself that in order to do thorough research on Thea, it was important for me to read her book.

I'd always been an extremely fast reader, so I finished in a few hours. Then I downloaded the next one in the series.

More research.

Several hours later, a knock on my office door startled me out of Thea's fictional world once again. My work involved a lot of intense focus and, often, very sensitive information. If I wasn't in my office when working, then I was in the SCIF—or Sensitive Compartmented Information Facility—also called a skiff room. So everyone knocked before entering, even my superiors.

That gave me time to hide away my e-reader before I called out for them to enter.

It was King and Blaze, the president and VP of my MC. They'd just been in a meeting with Echo and wanted to fill me in. After they left, I was tempted to go back to Thea's books, but I had shit to do. Reluctantly, I went back to my deep dive on

Violet and put together a dossier, then sent it to Echo in a secure email.

Two days later, I'd devoured two more of Thea's books and was downloading the next one when I got a text from Echo. Jeff, the guy we were surveilling, was on the phone with some associates, and he wanted me to monitor the trap and trace we'd set up. Unfortunately, we only learned about a meeting set for the next day.

I texted with the prez during the call, and we set up a plan.

When Jeff hung up, Echo's number immediately flashed on my cell phone screen.

"You get it?" he asked when I answered on the first ring.

"Too many relays," I replied with a frustrated grunt. "These fuckers aren't messing around. Whoever is in charge has deep pockets."

"Dammit," he muttered. "We'll have to put a tail on both of them after their meeting."

"Already on it," I assured him as I worked through the little information we'd gained from Jeff and his associate. It wasn't much, but I had produced results with less. "Sent a text to Prez, and he's sending Ink and Shadow to go with you."

Both men were club enforcers and knew how to

stay out of sight. Shadow had picked up his skills as a former thief, and Ink had ties to the southern mafia, who'd given him many skills that came in very handy.

"Kevlar and Cross are comin' to guard your woman," I added. Kevlar was our sergeant at arms, and Cross was our captain. They were both big guys who were exceptionally talented with weapons and had backgrounds in mixed martial arts.

"Great," he replied. "Tell Ink and Shadow to meet me at the library at eleven thirty."

"Got it."

During the time leading up to the meeting, I continued pursuing information about anyone and anything that might have been connected to Jeff and the people he worked with and for. When I dug up some new financial documents, I sent them to our treasurer, Ace, to do some forensic accounting magic.

The man was brilliant with money and kept the MC accounts more than flush. However, he'd been given his road name because of his gambling. He was a fucking ace and rarely lost. He'd cleaned out several patches while he'd been a prospect. It wasn't an addiction, though—he knew when to stop, and he wasn't reckless. Which only contributed to his lethal talent with the cards. He was very, very good.

Something was off about the businesses, but we hadn't yet figured out exactly what it was. Then some clues began to take shape as we realized that several of the shell companies were more likely to be owned by a woman. Since we'd recently discovered that women were not the only targets of this group, it made sense that the boss, Gene, would have a female among the higher-ups.

But when Jeff's meeting was over, we had brothers on his tail and on the associates he'd met with.

To our shock, it turned out that the person in charge spelled their name J-E-A-N, rather than G-E-N-E. The boss was a motherfucking woman.

This new insight into the ring gave me a fuck of a lot more to work with and a new player to assess. I told the boys to give me twenty-four hours—give or take a few hours—to put together everything I could find with all the information I'd already gathered.

Jean turned out to be a highly intelligent woman. And a rich, spoiled, high society bitch who was as cold as ice and meticulously careful. She had daddy and mommy issues and a clear dissatisfaction with the silver spoon she'd been born with in her mouth. So she took advantage of people—not because she needed their money but because she could.

When I had what I needed, I conferred with Ace, then we called a meeting.

King, Blaze, Ace, Ink, Shadow, Kevlar, Cross, and I were all in King's office when Echo arrived. We were sitting at the conference table to the right of the door, and he grabbed one of the other chairs and sat down, ending any conversations happening around him.

"Wizard?" King prompted.

I pushed a folder in each of their directions, then leaned back in my chair and tapped the keyboard of my laptop, where I had all of the same information pulled up in front of me. "That's pretty much everything we know about this group," I said, beginning the briefing. "There's also a chart for the hierarchy and an info sheet on each of the key players."

I walked them through everything, with Ace jumping in from time to time while mulling it all over in my head. From the thoughtful expressions on everyone's faces, I had a feeling we were all digesting the information and forming ideas about where to go from here.

When I finished, they asked several questions before we began to brainstorm. Suggestions were tossed out randomly while some of us analyzed the data more thoroughly and worked the problem from every angle we could see, attempting to come up with a plausible solution.

"Hold up," Shadow murmured, staring at one of the sheets of paper in his hand. "Jean has been married six times?"

I nodded. "Younger men. No prenup." Honestly, from everything I'd learned about her, I was a little surprised that they were all still alive. Jean definitely seemed like the Black Widow type.

"She was already filthy rich when she started this shit?" Kevlar blurted, tossing his folder on the table with a disgusted huff.

"Yup," I replied, with a pop on the P.

"She does it for the thrill then," Shadow surmised.

"Fair assumption," King agreed, his gaze locked on Shadow. "You think it would work?"

"Would what work?" Ink asked, his eyes darting back and forth between the two of them.

"Maybe," Echo grunted. "Only if there is a compelling reason for her to get back in the game."

I stopped typing and frowned as I tried to puzzle out the cryptic conversation.

"The fuck are you three *not* talking about?" snapped Blaze, voicing my thoughts.

Shadow scratched his chin, then set down his

folder and tapped his finger on it. "If we want to take down the entire organization, we have to get Jean. Not just the underlings because she'll just hire new ones."

"We need to catch her in a con," Echo added as he sat back and propped an ankle on the opposite knee.

"Exactly," Shadow agreed.

King folded his arms over his chest and leaned back against his chair. "How do we get her back in the game?"

"Bait," Cross tossed out. "A fish so big and illusive that she can't help herself."

"Appeal to her ego and her love of the thrill," Echo mused.

Ace rapped his knuckles on the table twice, then snatched my laptop out of my hands.

"What the hell?!" I bellowed in outrage.

Everyone stared at Ace, absolutely dumbfounded at his temerarious action. Touching my equipment was tantamount to treason in my mind. And the motherfucker had just stolen it. He was a dead man.

"Chill the fuck out, man," Ace said distractedly as he quickly typed. "Not like I stole your kidney or something."

I was so irate that I couldn't even form a sentence. My face was probably turning purple as I seethed, glaring at Ace venomously. My hands curled into fists so tight my knuckles turned white and cracked.

"You gonna save his ass?" I heard Echo ask quietly. Probably to Blaze, who was sitting next to him.

"Nah," Blaze responded lazily. "Fifty says Ace ends up in the hospital tonight."

A pretty safe bet, I thought.

There were several murmured agreements, and King chuckled, making me glance at him with astonishment.

He watched the two of us with amusement, something we rarely saw from the prez unless he was with his old lady or son.

"You have a death wish, Ace?" Cross murmured, watching me warily from the treasurer's other side.

He grunted and tapped hard on one key, then slid the laptop back over in front of me. Saving his life for the moment.

Taking a deep breath, I slid my eyes to my computer screen and scanned it. Irritation bloomed in my gut when I had to grudgingly admit, "This is good." Then I gave him another death glare and snarled, "Not gonna save you from being stabbed in your sleep when you're least expecting it, though."

Ace rolled his eyes. "It will if you want my help with the financial shit."

Fuck. Knowing I'd never decipher all that crap by myself, I ground my teeth into dust so I wouldn't say anything else.

"You two done?" King grunted, his face back in its usual scowl.

Ace gestured to the computer and explained, "Wizard and I have the beginnings of several aliases set up for cases when we need to get someone gone fast."

The Hounds of Hellfire were known for our ability to make people disappear...for a price. Not the hired killer kind of disappear, though. We gave people a new life. Under the right circumstances, we did it for free, but mostly, it was the MC's main source of income. Seeing as how we had experts in all the fields necessary for that kind of shit—a wizard at the tech stuff (hence my road name), a forger, a money guy, etc., etc., etc.

We'd long ago learned that it was helpful to have some of the legwork already done for several identities in case it was an emergency that required an immediate extraction.

"One of them is for a high roller," Ace explained further. "Someone who wants to disappear with their fortune and can afford to pay us to do it since it takes a fuck ton of work."

I nodded. "Won't take much work to get this up and running. The backend is as solid as they get. Breaking this identity would take years for the best of the best. Once it's live, we filter word of the new man through the grapevine, and as long as we're reading her right, she'll bite."

"Volunteers?" Ace asked with a smirk.

Echo sighed. "It's my op, so I'll do it."

Blaze and King shared a look, then they both grinned and King suggested, "Bring Violet in here to tell her."

Oh, that'll be good. I highly doubted Violet was gonna let her man date another woman, even if it was pretend.

"Why?" Echo questioned with narrowed eyes.

"Protection," Blaze drawled.

Echo scowled. "Why would Violet need protection?"

I hid my laugh in a cough, but the dirty look Echo shot my way told me I hadn't done a good job.

"Not Violet, Echo," King muttered as he stood

and walked around his desk to take a seat behind it. "You."

"What?" Echo shook his head, clearly confused.

Blaze swept his hand around the table and grunted. "Out."

Disappointed at missing what was bound to be a fantastic spectacle, we all protested but shut up and left when King growled. "Now!"

Later, we were sprawled out in the lounge of the clubhouse, drinking and taking a break from all the shit we were currently mired in.

Courtney, Blaze's old lady, was teasing Echo about how he'd basically forced his way into Violet's life after overhearing her narrating a book.

"Stalker much?" she asked with a giggle, making Blaze shake his head with a sigh.

Echo shrugged. "A guy's gotta do what he's gotta do to get his woman's attention."

"Damn straight," King agreed, cupping the back of his son's head with a soft smile that had his woman, Stella, blushing.

I shrugged and commented, "I'm sure some light stalking wouldn't scare Violet off after she narrated that book for Thea Drummond with the hero who took his masked stalker rep very seriously."

The room went silent as we all turned to gawk at me.

Oh shit.

Violet's eyes were wide as she asked, "You're familiar with *The Monster Behind the Mask?*"

Thinking fast, I said carelessly, "Stumbled across it when I was looking into you."

The comment turned Violet's attention back to Echo, and I should have simply left it at that...but when King got defensive about his ability to sweet-talk Stella, I couldn't help murmuring, "Chill, Prez." Then I shot a wicked smile at Echo. "At least you don't need to worry about your woman recording sex scenes with another guy."

Watching the ensuing argument was hilarious as fuck.

Eventually, Ace elbowed me in the side. "Another one bites the dust," he joked.

So it seemed.

My thoughts turned to Thea, and I felt a trickle of relief that I wouldn't have to worry about her working with another man—in any capacity. And I'd be the one she used to research any steamy scenes in her books.

I shook my head. "When I claim my woman, I'm

not gonna be pussy-whipped enough for her to act out hot-as-fuck sex scenes with another guy," I stated.

"Quit starting shit," King rumbled. "I read somewhere that babies are sensitive to their environment. Don't need Cadell to get all worked up." His face softened when he glanced at his newborn son.

But even though I hadn't been trying to make a dig, just a statement of fact, I raised my hands in a gesture of surrender. "Sorry, Prez."

Cadell suddenly let out a little wail. Everyone turned their attention to the baby, leaving me free to down the rest of my beer and grab another one from behind the long bar.

I thought about Echo's comment to Violet about falling for her when he saw her picture.

It seemed Ace was right. Another one had bitten the dust. But it wasn't Echo.

1

WIZARD

In a stroke of luck, we didn't need to burn one of the identities that Ace and I had prepped. Our club secretary had the perfect background to be Jean's next target.

Ash had been born into a wealthy family, the only child of a Texas politician. I was pretty sure they'd only had a kid because it polled well with his constituents.

Amazingly, Ash hadn't grown into a spiked douche or an empty suit like his dad. He'd aced school and earned scholarships that paid for his undergrad and law degrees. He'd worked for anything else he needed and never took a dime from his sorry excuse for parents.

When he became a public defender, I'd bet his

parents were horrified, but they played the proud parents. Then Ash found his real family with the Hounds of Hellfire. Despite our code of honor, we didn't always play on the right side of the law. We had our own brand of justice, and sometimes it put us in sticky situations. More often than not, Ash was the reason no one could nail us for any shady shit we were involved in.

Not surprisingly, he lost touch with the senator and his wife.

All of this put us in the perfect spot to carry out our plan. Ash was playing up his role as the senator's son—we'd spread the news that he'd been a recluse during the years since he dropped out of the media. The story was backed by people whose word and reputation were irrefutable.

It was fucking hilarious when Ash's parents called, suddenly wanting to reconnect. Clearly, they'd thought he was returning to society and wanted to take advantage of the situation or clean it up, depending on his motives. He promptly told them to go fuck themselves.

Ash had been against resurrecting his former self, but understanding what was at stake, he'd eventually agreed.

I'd secretly sighed in relief. My background

wasn't all that different from his although I'd been disowned by my shallow parents the first time I was arrested for hacking a government database.

Since I was only ten, they'd shipped me off to a boarding school in New York. I hadn't seen them since.

The father of one of my friends was a member of the Hounds of Hellfire. Gage told me to get my act together...or at least, not get caught. Then he treated me like another son, loving me like a father should, including busting my ass when I did stupid shit.

Having grown up around the club, I'd known I would prospect since I was a teenager. But Gage wouldn't hear of it until I'd finished college. By the time I was eighteen, I had my bachelor's, so I was able to prospect as soon as I was old enough.

Federal agencies often hired me as a civilian contractor, which was how I met King. He lured me out to Georgia and was one of the only two people in this branch of the MC who knew my real background.

Luckily, Ash was a much better candidate for this job.

Getting him established and keeping the charade going without a hitch took a fuck ton of work. So it didn't seem like a good time to begin something with

Thea. I wanted to be able to devote all of my time to her. So I tried to keep from going insane by reading every one of her books...and setting up a little surveillance of my own.

Being a genius—particularly in my field—had its perks.

But after two weeks, I'd reached the limit of my patience. I decided it was time to take action.

Sometimes gritty, badass bikers were as gossipy as teenage girls. I didn't want or need their interference or jokes. So I chose not to capitalize on her friendship with Violet and orchestrated my own "accidental" meeting with Thea instead.

I remembered she had an event in her calendar in a few days. A signing at a small bookstore.

Violet was on lockdown while we worked on taking down the group of conmen due to her involvement, which meant she wouldn't be joining Thea. It was perfect.

My woman was even more incredible in person. She was exactly as I'd imagined her, except her eyes twinkled and her smile was fucking brilliant. Her fans were clearly enchanted by her, something I completely understood.

For most of the evening, I stood off to the side, just observing. At one point, our eyes met, and when

I grinned, she blushed and stumbled over her words. It was adorable.

Near the end of the event, I stepped away to buy a few of her books, and when I returned, she glanced in my direction and blushed again.

Finally, the event began winding down, and as she stood to pack up, I swaggered over to the table.

"Hey there, gorgeous," I greeted her with my most charming smile.

"Um, hello," she replied softly. Her gaze dropped to my hands, and she raised her brow when she met my eyes again. "Did you want me to sign those?" The skepticism in her voice didn't really surprise me.

I was a huge guy in jeans, motorcycle boots, a white T-shirt, and my cut. Plus, I had tattoos wrapping around part of my left arm and more ink peeking out from the V-neck of my shirt.

Not her typical reader.

"Absolutely," I said with a wink, setting the books on the table.

She gave me a half smile and sat back down in her chair. "Do you want them made out to"—she glanced at the name stitched on my cut—"Wizard? Or just signed."

"To Baylor," I replied.

Her brow rose once more, and I chuckled, shaking my head. "Gets worse."

"Oh?" Her green eyes sparked with amusement.

"Chadwick."

"Pardon?"

I sighed. "Baylor Chadwick."

Thea covered her mouth to hide her giggle.

"Can only assume that my parents were trying to give me thick skin."

Smiling, she ducked her head and opened the first book. "To Baylor, it is."

I watched her hand move gracefully over the page and thought about what it would feel like gliding over my skin. Or wrapped around my dick. Before I became noticeably aroused, I switched to a much more benign train of thought.

When Thea finished, she picked up a small tote bag with her logo on it and slipped the books inside before handing it to me.

"Thanks."

She inclined her head and gave me a small smile. "You're welcome. It was nice to meet you, Baylor."

"Wouldn't really call this a meeting, baby."

Her brow puckered. "I don't understand."

"Meeting implies more than you signing my name."

"Okay, I'll bite." It was my turn to raise my brow, but despite the pink in her cheeks, her sigh was clearly one of disappointment. "What is your idea of 'meeting' someone?"

"Well, to truly become acquainted, you'd have to let me take you out to dinner."

Someone behind me sighed dreamily, and I fought the impulse to turn around and scare whoever it was away. To most people, I was very intimidating. My size and fierce scowl served me well in the right situations.

"I'm flattered," Thea said softly, "but I don't think it's a good idea."

The corners of my mouth turned down. "Why not?"

"I just...um...I don't date."

Her expression was stoic, but the flash of sadness in her eyes disturbed me. A bad experience? I hated the idea of someone hurting her, and I quelled the instinct to demand their name or names so I could hunt them down and kill them.

I was about to push a little harder when something told me it was the wrong tactic. For now, I'd slowly wear her down, then when the time was right, I'd move in fast and hard.

"How about this?" I suggested with a lopsided

smile. "I'll go for now. But I reserve the right to try to change your mind."

Thea giggled. "Just how do you intend to do that? You don't even know me."

"That's the point, isn't it?" I teased.

"I suppose you have a point, but I still don't see how you can convince me when you don't even know how to contact me."

I winked. "I have my ways, baby. Gonna sweep you off your feet eventually."

Thea's smile dimmed, and she muttered something under her breath. It sounded like, "That's what they all say," and my eyes narrowed.

"I don't know who 'all' is, baby, but I'm the only man you'll think of from now on."

Bending forward, I put a hand under her chin and raised her face. My thumb brushed softly over her lips, and I was pleased to see the glint of heat in her eyes.

"Later, baby."

I stared into her eyes for another moment, then reluctantly released her and ambled away.

2

THEA

The man whose butt I was doing my best not to stare at as he walked away from my signing table looked as though he could've modeled for as many romance book covers as he wanted. Mafia, motorcycle club, assassin—he was the living embodiment of the morally grey heroes romance readers loved. Me included.

Thinking about his short, dark hair, brown eyes, chiseled jaw that was covered in scruff, and kissable lips, I wanted to kick my own butt for the answer I had given him.

At only five feet and two inches, I was used to pretty much everyone being taller than me. But he had to have more than a full foot on me since I'd needed to crane my neck all the way back to stare up at him.

My cheeks heated as I briefly considered the things he could do to me in bed with our height disparity. With his lean muscles, I had no doubt that he'd easily be able to hold me against the wall like I'd done in several scenes that I'd written. Even better, he could probably put me exactly where he wanted me—and test out any position I wanted to write into a story.

I loved being a romance author. I was literally living my dream...except for one small problem. My dating life was nonexistent.

It was difficult to trust men who asked me out when so many of them did it in a creepy way. I couldn't even count the number of times that a guy suggested we skip dinner and head back to his place...before we even went out on one date.

It was as though they all assumed that just because I wrote steamy sex scenes in my books, I had to be a nymphomaniac or something. Little did they know that reality was the furthest thing from what they thought. Not that I advertised that I was a virgin. My lack of a sex life was nobody's business but my own.

I'd never had a problem turning one of them down. Until today.

Baylor Chadwick was my every fantasy come to life. Not accepting his offer had been more difficult than attending my first signing—which was saying a lot since I'd never been more nervous than that day.

"Please tell me that I heard wrong, and you did not just turn that hunk of a man down."

I glanced up at the woman who I hadn't realized was behind Baylor that whole time. My signing time was already done, but I hated to turn away readers. Although her nosiness tempted me to do just that, I pasted on a smile and shook my head. "Sorry, but yes. It's sad but true. I had to turn him down."

She pressed her hands together, eyes going wide. "Ooh, is it because he's going to be the model on the cover you're supposed to reveal next month? If so, don't be worried about blurring the line. Other authors have dated cover models before. Heck, I know of one author/model couple who got married. You never know where you'll meet your very own happily ever after."

"You make an excellent point." The smile I flashed her held none of my usual warmth, but she didn't seem to notice. "I'll definitely keep that in mind."

"You really should. That man looked as though he could inspire sex scenes that are even hotter than the ones you've already published. And considering I always tell my friends that you write my favorite spicy scenes, that's saying a lot."

As she fanned herself, the guy behind her stepped to the side to stand next to her. Glancing up from the book I'd just snagged from the pile so I could sign it for her, it took a moment to realize I recognized him.

"Oh my goodness," I gasped, getting to my feet. "I had no idea you'd be here, Mark. You should've let me know so you didn't get stuck standing in line."

The woman's head whipped to the right so fast I was worried she might've hurt herself when she gasped. But she proved me wrong when she sputtered, "Wait, I know you. You're Mark Winter, the audiobook narrator. Oh my gosh, would you sign my book too, please? You did such a great job bringing the hero to life."

Mark flashed me an inquiring smile as though he was asking for my permission before agreeing. When I nodded, he murmured, "Sure."

After sitting back down to scribble a quick note and sign her book, I handed it to him. Getting his signature didn't stop her from pushing the issue of Baylor asking me out again. And this time, she pulled Mark into it.

Nudging his side with her elbow, she asked, "Don't you think Thea should have said yes to the date with that hot-as-sin guy? Opportunities like that don't come along every day."

Mark's gaze darted toward me, irritation clear in his eyes. I figured he had more than his fair share of similar interactions with fans. The majority of his narrations were romance titles, and he had attended some book events on his own and with other authors. Although his looks didn't do anything for me, I wouldn't be surprised if readers had asked him out at them since he was attractive.

"I think Thea knows her own mind and should only go out with someone she's truly interested in."

"I suppose you're right," the reader muttered as she accepted the signed book from him.

As she walked away, I patted the stack of paperbacks in front of me and smiled at Mark. "Thanks for backing me up. I'm surprised to see you here, though. Didn't you already get a signed copy from the production company?"

"Sure did," he confirmed with a grin. "But I live a

couple of towns over and heard that you'd be here, so I figured I would stop in to show my support for my favorite author."

I shook my head with a laugh. "Only because I've hired you so often."

"Don't sell yourself short." He rapped his knuckles against the table. "I guess I better let you get back to packing up. Looking forward to our next project."

"Thanks for stopping by." I had no idea he lived nearby since I paid him through the production company that I used and had never bumped into him before.

Situations like this reminded me how small the world really was. Something that was proved true with how often I ran into Baylor over the next week. He seemed to be almost everywhere I went. It felt as though the universe was testing the limits of my self-control when it came to him because he used every opportunity to ask me on a date. Including now, in the middle of the produce section at the grocery store.

"Those look juicy."

My head jerked up at the sound of the now-familiar masculine voice. I would have dropped the grapefruit I held, except Baylor steadied my hand before it slipped from my fingers.

"Sorry, I didn't mean to startle you."

I narrowed my eyes at him. "Then you should stop sneaking up on me."

He snatched a grapefruit from the bin and tossed it into the air, catching it with a smirk. "Didn't realize you were so focused on picking out the perfect piece of fruit and didn't hear me come up behind you."

My cheeks heated as I thought about the creative way I'd used a grapefruit in a book I wrote last year. They turned even pinker when I spotted the gleam in Baylor's brown eyes and wondered if he'd read that blow job scene and was remembering the same thing. It seemed impossible to think that this huge, tough-looking guy who was a member of a motorcycle club actually read romance novels, though. So I shook off my suspicion as I dropped my fruit into a plastic bag before placing it in my basket.

"I guess I better work on my situational awareness," I muttered.

"You really should. A woman can never be too careful," he agreed with a nod. "If you want some self-defense pointers, I can help you out with that. I'm even free tonight."

"Sorry, but no."

I kept my refusal short because I wasn't sure I could stop myself from accepting if I said too much.

"That's okay, baby. I'll keep working for a yes. You're more than worth it."

His parting words stuck with me, making it even more difficult to turn him down the next time he asked. And all of the other times after, too.

3

WIZARD

It had been a very fucking long two weeks since I dropped into Thea's signing. I'd done my best to convince her to go out with me, but she was proving to be more stubborn than I expected.

I'd even managed to pop in on her when she was out of the house a few times. Of course, I always had an excuse for being there. She'd still avoided agreeing to a date, but I learned more about her every time. I was even more convinced that she was the perfect woman for me. And she was losing steam in her rejections.

Still, my attention was more distracted than she deserved, so I hadn't pushed any harder.

Tonight, Echo and I were staked out at a hotel, monitoring Ash on his date with Jean. Even though we were in the home stretch, I was in a shitty mood and was taking it out on Ash by being an ass and ribbing him endlessly through our comms. It was stupid, but I was blowing off steam.

When Ash finished giving Jean what she needed to break into his house, Echo had someone rush into the ballroom and tell him that his dad was in the hospital.

Ash managed to play the devastated son perfectly, and as he rushed from the room, I started a slow clap.

Echo rolled his eyes at me. "I'd be gone when he gets here if I were you."

I grinned and continued helping Echo pack up our shit.

"My dad in the hospital?" Ash scoffed as he stormed into the room, yanking off his bow tie. "You couldn't have come up with anything better? Do you know how fucking hard it was to pretend I cared?"

Echo shrugged. "Best I could think of to get you out fast while making sure she knew you wouldn't be home tonight. In an hour, send her a text to check in and let her know you'll be there for at least twenty-four hours."

They talked about our plans while I continued to set one of my computers into a special hard case.

After Ash had stripped out of his tux and pulled on a pair of jeans and a T-shirt, he turned to me with a scathing expression. "You and I need to have a talk, brother. Because if I didn't know better, I'd think you were trying to get your ass handed to you."

"He's just trying not to think about the woman who won't give him the time of day," Echo answered.

I snapped the case closed as I grunted, "You don't know what the fuck you're talking about." I added it to the equipment on the trolley that we used to bring it all up from our van. I glared at him as I pushed the cart to the door.

Echo smirked. "Violet and I have no secrets. You think she doesn't know what's going on with you and Thea?"

"We're not talking about this," I barked before slamming open the door and pushing the cart through it.

"Touchy," I heard Ash joke.

I growled in frustration but didn't engage, choosing to get the hell outta there instead.

Everything was finally done and wrapped up a few days later. Knowing that Thea liked to write at a specific coffee house some afternoons, I checked the parking lot. When I spied her car, I hopped on my bike and headed over there.

The bell dinged as I walked inside, and my gaze immediately went to Thea's preferred booth. She was focused intensely on her computer, her fingers tip-tapping the keyboard.

As I approached, her head popped up, almost like she sensed me, and when a slow smile spread across my face, pink bloomed on her cheeks.

"Hey, baby," I greeted as I scooted onto the bench seat right next to her.

"Hi," she replied softly, her full pink lips curling up sweetly. "What are you doing here?"

"Looking for you," I replied, going for full honesty this time. Now that she could have my full attention, and she'd had some time to get to know me, I was done playing around.

"Oh?" Her expression was simply curious, but the darkening of her blush and the way her eyes brightened gave away her pleasure at my confession.

"Sorry it's been a few days since we saw each other. Had club business to handle, and it was taking most of my time. It's taken care of now, and you have one hundred percent of my focus."

"Has it been a few days? I hadn't noticed," she said with an innocent blink.

I leaned in close until my lips would brush against her ear as I whispered, "Liar." Then I kissed the shell before adding, "You know you missed me as much as I missed you, baby."

Her breath hitched for a moment, making me smile. I inhaled deeply as I dragged my nose along her jaw. "You smell so fucking good," I groaned.

"Y-you missed me?" she gasped lightly.

I raised my head and captured her jaw, turning her head so our eyes met. "I've dreamed of you each and every damn night. My thoughts of you were the only bright spot, the one thing that kept me going during the darkest hours of my job."

Her mouth opened and closed a few times, indicating she was at a loss for words. Then she sputtered, "Did you...did you just quote *The Spy's Return?*"

I chuckled and winked. "More or less." I'd altered the last word, but the rest had been taken directly from her book.

"How...?" Shock washed over her face, and she asked softly, "You've read my book?"

Releasing her chin, I grinned as I sat back against the booth and slipped my arm around her waist, tucking her close into my side.

"Books," I corrected, emphasizing the S.

Thea double-blinked before her eyes grew wide. "How many?"

I lifted my free hand and counted to five under my breath, lifting a finger with each number.

"Five?" Her tone was astounded.

"Shhh. Still counting." I hushed her, then continued to count until I finally announced, "Eighteen."

Thea was quiet for a moment, her eyes wide as she stared up at me. "You've read them all?"

"Romance novels aren't only for women, you know," I joked.

She raised an eyebrow, and her gaze swept over me.

"Don't judge a book by its cover," I admonished, tongue in cheek.

Her head popped up to stare at me, then she burst into laughter. The sound was as beautiful as the rest of her. I could happily listen to it for the rest of my life...and whatever noises she made when she was coming.

"Romance novels aren't usually my thing," I admitted with a smile. "But you are a damn good writer, baby. Started the first one because I was curious, then I was hooked. Besides, it was a way to be close to you while I was so busy with club shit."

Thea's green orbs heated as her body practically melted into mine. "You win," she said softly.

"Oh?" I leaned in close until our breaths were mingling. "What did I win?"

Her gaze moved down to my chest, and her cheeks reddened. "I'll go on a date with you."

Triumph and satisfaction roared through me, but I kept my cool, not wanting to put her off by being too smug. "Tomorrow night?"

"Um, how about Friday?"

I lifted her chin and shook my head. "Tomorrow. Not gonna let you change your mind."

She giggled and nodded. "Tomorrow," she conceded. "We can meet for lunch."

I frowned. "That's not a date."

Thea huffed adorably. "Of course it is. That's why it's called a lunch *date*."

"Semantics."

"Take it or leave it, Baylor."

"Fine," I growled. "Lunch. I'll pick you up—"

"I'll meet you there," she interrupted.

Telling myself not to push, I swallowed my frustration and agreed. "Do you know where The Fuel & Flame Diner is?"

Thea's head tilted to the side, thinking for a beat. "Isn't that the place on Main Street? Across from Inferno Cycles and Customs?"

My brow rose. "You know our garage?"

Her cheeks flamed again, and she giggled. "One of my heroes specialized in custom motorcycles. I went there to do some research a couple of years ago. I talked to a guy...Cross, I think."

She'd met Cross? Why hadn't he told me? Jealousy burned in my chest until I forced myself to think rationally. He probably didn't even remember one random conversation with a woman. Though how anyone could forget Thea was a mystery to me.

"He was really nice and didn't even ask my name once I told him I was an author researching for a book."

The explanation I'd come up with seemed even more plausible with that information, cooling the fire inside me. It seemed I wouldn't have to kill my brother, which saved me a ton of shit with the club.

"Anyway. I'll meet you there at noon if that works for you?"

"Sure, baby," I confirmed. It was tempting to stay right where I was and spend more time with my woman. But I respected her job, and if she was anything like me, she probably wanted to be alone and free of distractions while she worked. "Much as I'd like to stay and be with you, I'm gonna let you get back to work."

"Thank you," she murmured. "I appreciate your understanding."

I nodded and briefly squeezed the arm I had around her before removing it. "I know you must have a deadline soon with the preorder you have up."

Thea's face turned soft again, and she smiled. "You really have read all of my books, haven't you?"

My tone was serious when I replied, "Never gonna lie to you, baby. I might have to censor what I tell you when it comes to club business, but I'll always be honest." I leaned in and kissed her forehead before scooting out of the booth. "See you tomorrow, baby."

When I reached the door, I glanced back and saw her watching me with a dreamy expression. It took a fuck of a lot of effort to walk away, but I reminded myself that I had eyes on her all the time. That would have to suffice for now.

4

THEA

"Are you almost there?" Violet asked.

"Yes, and I need you to tell me again that this was the right choice," I demanded, glaring at the red stoplight through my windshield.

Five days ago, I had finally confided in her about meeting Wizard and him asking me out—although I hadn't told her how often it had happened. She had told me that he was a great guy and urged me to give him a chance. Between her coaxing and finding out a few days later that he'd actually read my books and not just the sex scenes, I finally agreed to our date today.

Now that I was actually on my way to meet him, I was having second thoughts. The kind that told me to turn the car around and go back home because I was way too nervous to actually go through with my first real date.

"You're going to have an amazing time even though you would only agree to lunch, which is kind of lame for a first date."

Her teasing relieved some of my nervousness and made me giggle. "Like you have any room to judge. Echo is the only guy you've ever gone out with, and where did you guys go on your first date? Your apartment? Does that even count?"

"Fair point," she conceded.

"I'm going to assume what you meant to say was that my first date with Baylor is much more normal than how you and Echo started your relationship," I quipped, turning into the parking lot and pulling into a spot near the front door of the diner.

Violet laughed. "You're the famous romance author, so I guess I'll let you stick with that story if it makes you happy."

"Hardly famous." I snorted, shaking my head.

"Quit arguing with me and get in there," she ordered. "I'm sure Wizard is already waiting."

It was weird to hear Violet use his road name, but I guessed it was even odder to her that I used his real name since bikers tended to limit how many people were allowed to do that. Something I hadn't considered until now.

"I'll call you when I'm headed back home."

"Don't rush. Enjoy your date!"

I tucked my phone in my purse and climbed out of my car. Violet was proved correct in her prediction that Baylor would be waiting for me when I walked through the door and spotted him at a booth in the back corner.

As though sensing I was near, his head lifted, and he stood. I wasn't aware of anything other than the intensity of his dark gaze as I made my way over. When I got close, he stepped out of the booth and guided me into his spot. Then he nudged me over to sit next to me.

Pointing across from us, I murmured, "There's a whole other half to this booth."

"Yup." At my questioning look, he added, "Took me too damn long to get you to agree to this date. Now that I have you here, I don't want to let you get too far."

"Oh." I usually had no problem thinking of something witty to say, but his words left me nearly speechless. It sounded exactly like something I would've written for one of my heroes.

"You good with me here?" he asked.

I flashed him a shy smile. "Yeah."

The server stopped next to our booth, interrupting our moment. "Hey, Wizard. Now that your woman has joined you, are you ready to order?"

I wasn't surprised she knew Baylor since this place was so close to his club's garage. Judging by how she spoke to him, I assumed he came here often. Turning to him, I asked, "Which burger is the best?"

"The smash burger with cheese if you like to go the traditional route, or the biker barbecue if you're good with onion strings, tangy sauce, and bacon."

"Yum." I licked my lips and grinned. "Sounds perfect."

"Two with fries?" the server asked.

"Sounds good to me," Baylor confirmed.

She nodded before her attention switched back to me. "And to drink?"

"Ginger ale, please."

"You got it."

After she left, I shifted in the booth to face Baylor with my left elbow on the table and my right knee pressed against the back of the booth. "Please tell me the burgers are as good as they sound."

"Even better."

We talked about our favorite foods—spaghetti for me and tacos for him—while we waited for our order.

The conversation flowed easily from there, and before I knew it, we'd devoured our burgers and fries.

Leaning back against the booth, I patted my belly. "Wow, you weren't kidding about how amazing those were."

"I'll do you one even better when I take you for dinner tomorrow night. Italian."

I quirked a brow at him. "I don't remember agreeing to a second date yet."

"This one went too well for you to turn me down again. Especially when I'm offering up the best spaghetti Riverstone has to offer." His smirk was sexy enough to make my panties spontaneously combust. "Does six work for dinner tomorrow night?"

I beamed a smile at him. "Well, since you asked so nicely..."

He shook his head with a deep laugh. "Was that what I was doing wrong all this time? I shoulda just told you what time I was taking you out?"

"Nah, that definitely wouldn't have worked until now."

"I figured." He chuckled again. "But I sure as shit am not gonna argue when you finally agreed to dinner."

"Tomorrow at six," I confirmed with a soft smile.

With that settled, he stood and held a big hand

out to me. "And this time, I'm gonna pick you up at home."

"I'll allow that," I agreed with a shiver as his warm palm slid against mine.

"Good."

We walked hand in hand to my car, where I let out the slightest whimper of disappointment when he dropped his arm. I realized Baylor heard it when he grunted, "Fuck it," and cupped my cheeks with his hands. My lips parted on a gasp as his mouth crashed against me, and his tongue slid inside to tangle with mine.

My first real kiss was taking place in the parking lot of a diner, but I couldn't have written it better. Where we were didn't matter...only the melting sensation I felt as he explored the cavern of my mouth. I'd never experienced the feeling of butterflies swirling in my belly until now. And I never wanted it to end.

Unfortunately, reality reared its ugly head in the form of somebody laying on their horn as they drove past. Baylor lifted his head to glare at them, and the moment was over much sooner than I would have liked.

While I shook off the sensual fog from his kiss, he helped me into the car and secured my belt. Then he patted the hood and murmured, "Drive safe, baby."

The first thing I did after I pulled out of the parking lot was call Violet.

"So...how was it?" she asked, without bothering to greet me.

"Amazing." I let out a dreamy sigh before telling her everything that had happened during my date.

As I pulled into the driveway of the little house I rented, she boasted, "See, I was right when I told you to put the poor guy out of his misery."

I shook my head with a laugh while I parked. "There isn't a single thing about Baylor that makes him even the tiniest bit deserving of your pity. He's built like a Greek god, is way smarter than I expected, belongs to a motorcycle club, and is sexier than any one man deserves to be."

She giggled. "Fair point."

I put my phone in speaker mode before turning off the engine of my car. Climbing out, I stumbled to a stop after I only took two steps forward. "Oh, crap."

"What's wrong?" Violet asked. "Did you get a coffee to go and spill all over yourself?"

"I only did that once," I huffed, regretting that I told her that story.

"If that's not the problem, what is?"

I cautiously approached my front steps, scanning up and down the sidewalk and street to make sure nobody was watching. After I confirmed that I was alone, I crouched down to peer more closely at the bouquet on my porch.

"Thea, what in the world is going on?" Violet squealed through my phone.

Heaving a deep sigh, I muttered, "I got flowers."

"Awww, Baylor brought you a bouquet for your first date? That is so sweet, and I have to admit, also super surprising. He deserves major brownie points for thinking of that."

For a moment, I considered the possibility that they were from Baylor, but I quickly discarded it. If he'd wanted to give me flowers, he would've brought them to the coffee house. "No, they're not from him."

"Who in the heck sent them then?" she demanded.

I waited until I tugged the card from the bouquet and scanned the message written in black ink on it. This wasn't the first note I'd received, but it was definitely the scariest.

"I think I have a stalker."

5

WIZARD

I had a lot of work to do when I returned to the clubhouse, so I dove into it, looking for a distraction. Otherwise, I would have spent the rest of the day and tomorrow morning obsessively watching Thea.

A few hours later, there was a knock on my office door, and I frowned at the interruption. "What?" I called out, quickly minimizing the files I was studying since they were confidential.

The door opened, and Echo walked inside, shutting it behind him. "Just talked to Violet," he told me as he dropped onto the couch I had across from my desk and wall of computer screens. I'd dragged it in there after falling asleep in my chair a few times while waiting for a ping on something I was searching for.

My eyes narrowed. "Wouldn't be here to talk to me about your old lady unless it has to do with Thea," I surmised.

He ran his hands through his hair and blew out a breath. "Just keep your shit together while I tell you everything."

Not a good sign. "Then spit it the fuck out," I snapped.

"Violet was on the phone with Thea when she got home today. Seems there were flowers and a note on her doorstep."

My hands balled into fists, and the green monster clawed at my chest. "From who?" I demanded in a lethal tone.

"Don't know. It was the first Violet had heard about the situation, and she came right to me when she found out."

"A stalker?"

Echo nodded. "That's the conclusion Thea came to, as well. Mostly because this note was an escalation."

"A fucking escalation from what?" I bellowed, jumping to my feet.

"Like I said, Violet was in the dark, so she didn't

know much. But she's worried, so she asked me to tell you."

I couldn't talk through the fury engulfing me, so I gave him a chin lift before grabbing my shit and stalking out to my truck. Thea was coming back with me whether she wanted to or not, so I needed a vehicle that could bring some of her stuff.

On the drive to her house, I tried to talk myself down into a calmer state. I needed to convince Thea to leave with me and let me protect her. A logical argument and firm request were probably the best way to go. But by the time I arrived, I was still fuming and ready to just throw her over my shoulder and take her somewhere safe. Even if she kicked and screamed the whole way.

"Thea!" I shouted as I pounded on her door.

When she opened it a minute later, I scowled. "Never answer the fucking door without finding out who it is first!" I growled.

She pointed at her doorbell and muttered, "I have a camera."

Not in the mood to be soothed, I just grunted in response. Placing a hand on her stomach, I urged her to move backward until I was able to step inside.

She backed up a few feet more and crossed her

arms over her chest, sighing, "Violet tattled, didn't she?"

I closed the distance between us and glared down at her. "She shouldn't have had to, Thea. You should have told me yourself."

"Why would I tell you?" she argued. "It's not like you're my boyfriend. We just had our first date!"

If I hadn't been so monumentally pissed, I would have taken a second to appreciate that she wasn't intimidated by our size difference, especially with my gritty personality and exterior.

"That might be true, baby, but if you think you haven't been mine since the day we met, you're lying to yourself."

She remained stubbornly silent, and I nodded. "That's what I thought."

After a slow, deep breath, she spoke. "It wasn't a big deal before. Just some flowers and poetic notes. It seemed harmless enough."

My brow rose to my hairline. "Ignoring the fact that those actions were signs that this fucker was a stalker. They were being delivered to your fucking house, Thea. That alone should've sent you to Echo or the police."

She frowned and jammed her hands onto her hips. "They won't deliver flowers to a PO Box,

Baylor. I have a service that delivers those kinds of things so I don't have to give out my real address."

It was a solid explanation, but it didn't sit right with me. "Let me see the note," I muttered, stalking past her into her bright, open living room. My computer bag was slung over my shoulder, so I set it on the coffee table before taking a seat in a comfortable armchair.

She stared at me in confusion, and I canted my head. "The note, baby," I urged again, trying not to sound quite as gruff. I must have succeeded because she dropped her arms to her sides and walked toward the kitchen.

The two rooms were separated by a bar with two stools tucked in from the living room side.

As I opened my laptop, I heard a drawer opening and papers rustling. Then I glanced up when her footsteps headed in my direction. She held out a notecard and a printed sheet of paper.

"Thanks, baby." I set the items down next to my computer, noting the name of the nursery where the flowers had been ordered from. "This is the one from today?"

"Yes."

Glancing up at her, I asked, "Where are the rest?"

"The rest?" she echoed.

"Might think I don't know you, baby, but you're very wrong. Even though you didn't want to believe it, somewhere deep down, you knew the person sending you shit could be a stalker. Where are the other letters?"

Thea blinked at me, obviously startled by my accuracy. Finally, she mumbled, "In the drawer." She turned and hurried back to the kitchen while I did some unethical shit and broke a couple of laws to get the information I needed.

She handed me a manila envelope when she returned, and I set it next to the other note. Then I gave her a pointed look. "None of the deliveries were sent to your PO Box, Thea. They were sent directly to your address from the store."

"How could you possibly know that?" she asked, her tone skeptical. "Besides, they didn't all come from the same shop."

I'd hacked what I needed to make an intuitive leap to the other nurseries and checked all the deliveries sent to her address. "I'll explain it later, but for now, I just need you to trust me."

"Okay," she whispered as she sank into the chair next to mine.

I smiled in approval and picked up the note she'd

received after lunch. As I read, my expression turned into a dark, murderous scowl.

The stalker warned her that he was watching and had been waiting for the right moment. Now that she was "whoring" herself out to another man, he threatened to harm her if she didn't break it off. Then he ended it by softening his language and telling her about all the sex scenes she'd written that he couldn't wait to do in person rather than just dreaming about it. Some of the shit he wrote was explicit, and the paper nearly crumpled in my hand from my tight grip.

"Gonna kill this motherfucker," I gritted out through clenched teeth.

Thea's voice was hesitant when she commented, "Somehow, I don't think you're bluffing."

I turned my gaze to her face, shuttering some of my homicidal rage so I didn't scare the hell out of her. "Never bluffing when it comes to your safety, baby."

She sighed and pushed up to her feet. "I guess it's time to take this to the police."

"Not going to the cops," I informed her as I snapped my laptop closed and slipped it into my satchel. "Go pack a bag, baby. Make sure you have enough shit for a couple of weeks." I added the most recent letter to the envelope with the others and stuffed it next to my computer.

"Excuse me?" she uttered in a bewildered tone.

I stood to my full height, and once again, I moved close enough that she had to drop her head nearly all the way back to meet my gaze. "You heard me."

She shook her head. "Why do I need to pack a bag? And why aren't we going to the police?"

"Taking you back to the Hounds of Hellfire compound. Nowhere safer, and we'll do a hell of a lot better at catching this asshole." My smile was wicked when I added, "And we'll be the ones meting out his punishment."

Her eyes were heated and her cheeks ruddy when she hummed, "Ummm...I don't think...that's not..."

I grinned. Seemed my girl liked it when I was tough and growly. *Something to keep in mind.*

"Don't worry about it, baby. Now go pack a bag before I drag your sexy ass outta here without any of your shit. We're leaving in ten minutes."

She opened her mouth, most likely to argue with me, so I covered her lips with my own. The kiss was insistent, drugging, and I was close to losing control when I finally pulled back.

"Do as you're told, baby," I muttered, then I

turned her around by her shoulders and patted her ass to get her moving.

Dazed, she slowly walked away, her hips swaying. I kept my eyes glued to her ass. Damn, my woman was hot as fuck.

Ten minutes later, she hadn't come out of the bedroom, so I stalked down the hall to see what was taking her so long.

She was sitting on the bed, a medium-sized suitcase open beside her. Noting that it was filled to the brim, I decided we could talk about whatever was on her mind later. Right now, I wanted her in my room at the clubhouse where I knew she was safe. And I was done trying to talk her into the plan.

I closed her bag and zipped it up, then set it on the floor.

Bracing my feet apart, I crossed my arms over my chest and stared down at her. "Your ten minutes are up, baby."

"Baylor...I think—" She yelped when I bent down and picked her up, gently tossing her over my shoulder.

I grabbed her suitcase and marched out to the front door.

"What the heck?" she squawked.

"Gave you plenty of warning, baby," I growled. "Doing things my way now."

Once we were outside, I locked and shut her door. "Need a fucking alarm system," I grumbled as I made my way to the truck. Although she didn't need one in this place anymore. Now that she was living with me, I wasn't about to let her go.

When we reached the truck, I opened the back door and tossed her bag onto the bench seat in the extended cab. After slamming it shut, I opened the front passenger door and gently set Thea in the seat. She still seemed to be in a state of shock because she didn't speak or try to stop me from buckling her in.

The sound of the belt clicking into place resonated in the quiet of the truck. I was about to move away but stopped and grasped her chin, making sure we were eye to eye when I spoke again. "No more pushing me away, Thea," I told her. "You've got no choice but to have me in your life now. And not just because of the stalker. I'm done being patient. We are happening. End of story."

6

THEA

I should have protested more, but something about Baylor being all growly and possessive made me more agreeable than I should have been. Probably because it made him even sexier than usual. Which was saying a lot since he was the hottest guy I'd ever met, and I'd been around many male cover models that readers swooned over.

And if that wasn't enough to sway me, the swarm of butterflies in my belly at being told we were happening would've gotten me to agree.

As he backed his truck out of my driveway, I grumbled, "Maybe I was wrong."

"About what?"

I crossed my arms over my chest with a huff. "I thought that you reading my books was a really good thing...until you acted like one of my heroes, right down to what he'd say in a situation like this."

"You tellin' me that I'm better than the book boyfriends you write?" he asked, smirking.

I rolled my eyes. "I didn't say *better*."

"Mm-hmm," he hummed, the earlier tension gone from his muscular frame.

"Ugh, you're never going to let me live that down, are you?" I muttered. "Even though it is not at all what I said."

"But it's what I heard," he teased.

I tore my gaze away from the flexing of his forearms as he gripped the steering wheel, mentally cursing the fact that I found it so distracting. "You're awfully happy for a guy who was incredibly pissed off only ten minutes ago."

"Got every reason to be thrilled as fuck right now, baby." He dropped his hand to my thigh and gave it a comforting squeeze. "Gonna have you nearby around the clock, just like I've wanted for the past month."

"Except I still have a serious problem—my stalker," I reminded him.

"Like I told you, the club will take care of him. You don't need to worry about it anymore."

I had no doubt that he meant what he said.

Violet had been deliberately vague about how she and Echo had met, but she'd let it slip once that he had been in her building to look into her creepy neighbor. Since that guy had disappeared, I could only assume that my friend had been right about her impression of him. And that the Hounds of Hellfire had taken care of the situation, whatever it was.

"Thank you," I whispered.

Baylor had left his hand on my thigh, so he gave it another squeeze. "You have no need to thank me, baby. I'm the kind of man who takes care of what's his. And you are most definitely mine."

I barely resisted pressing my thighs together to ease the ache in my core, only because with his hand where it was, he'd know exactly what I was trying to do. "Seriously, you need to stop it with those one-liners that would make perfect teasers for my books."

He winked at me with a deep chuckle. "Can't help it if I'm one of your heroes come to life. And even if I could, I wouldn't."

"How come?"

"It took a lot of effort to get you to agree to our first date. So I'm gonna take every advantage I can get when it comes to you, baby," he explained, his dark eyes turning serious.

"There is just going to be no resisting you if you

insist on keeping that up," I mumbled, turning to stare out the passenger side window for the rest of the drive. The last thing I wanted was to arrive at the Hounds of Hellfire clubhouse for the first time with drenched panties.

He laughed again at my reaction but didn't say anything else until we pulled through the gates of the compound and parked.

While Baylor got my suitcase out of the back of the extended cab, I climbed out of the passenger seat. Glaring at me after he rounded the truck, he growled, "Next time, wait for me. I'll get your door."

That confirmed it. He was like my biker kryptonite, impossible to resist. I had a feeling it wasn't going to be long before I didn't have to worry about being a virgin romance author anymore. Not when I wanted to throw myself at Baylor every time he said something like that. Which was often.

"Will do."

I was very aware of the heat of his palm on my lower back as he led me inside the clubhouse. My gaze scanned the space, my lips curving into a grin when I realized it looked similar enough to the ones I had read—and written—about to feel comfortable to me. Then I spotted Violet and Echo at the far end of the bar, and their familiar faces eased my remaining nervousness.

Violet rushed over, her eyes filled with concern. Assuming her distress was twofold, I assured, "Don't worry. I'm not mad that you told Echo what's going on. And Baylor said he'll take care of my stalker, so there's no need to be freaked out. He's only known about the guy for like half an hour and already knows more than I do about the situation. He's got it under control."

"I'm sure he does," Echo agreed, wrapping his arm around Violet's shoulders.

Baylor mimicked his club brother's action, tugging me against his side. "Damn straight."

Violet rolled her eyes. "Want me to show you around while Wizard takes your stuff to his room?"

My breath caught in my throat at the realization that I wouldn't just be staying at the clubhouse while Baylor dealt with my stalker. I'd be sleeping in his room. With him, most likely.

Nodding, I murmured, "Um...yeah, that would be great."

"I'll meet you in the kitchen." Hefting my suitcase higher, he added, "It's been a while since we polished off those burgers. Need some fuel while I dig into this problem."

Violet crooked her arm through mine. "You have perfect timing. Ink made his mama's famous sauce and homemade pasta."

"Guess I'm treating you to your favorite meal sooner than we planned, baby." Baylor winked at me before walking away.

"Aw, you forgot to tell me that your second date was going to be Italian." Violet led me past the row of stools lining the bar and through a door that led to a huge kitchen. Several guys were seated at the tables but only two women, who both stood and hurried over to us.

"You must be Thea. I'm Courtney, Blaze's old lady," the one with black hair said as the guy she'd been sitting next to gave me a chin lift.

"And I'm Stella," the honey blonde added, jerking her thumb toward the other guy with dark hair. "King's old lady."

"Nice to meet you both," I replied, wondering how they already knew who I was.

By the time Violet and Echo finished introducing me to the other Hounds in the kitchen—Ink, Ace, Kevlar, and Edge—Baylor joined us.

"You need us?" King asked him.

"After I take care of my woman," he replied.

Their byplay was brief and cryptic, but it was

just enough for me to guess that his club president had already heard about my stalker. Although I was tempted to ask about it, I remembered what he'd told me about club business and always being honest with me. If I was going to be in a relationship with Baylor, I needed to fit into his world. Which meant trusting him to tell me what I needed to know...and that anything he kept secret wouldn't hurt me. So I kept my questions to myself while we enjoyed the best spaghetti I'd ever tasted.

"Thanks, Ink. That was delicious."

He waved off my gratitude. "Glad you enjoyed it, but the compliments really should go to my *mamma*. I just used her recipe."

"C'mon, baby." Baylor tugged me away from his club brother. "Gotta get you up to my room before I meet with the prez."

Since I was curious about his room, I didn't argue. When we got there, I was a little surprised by what I found. "No wall of monitors for when you do your tech stuff?"

"Not in here," he said as he closed the door behind us.

My suitcase was next to the open closet door, and there was another that was closed. "En suite bathroom?"

"Yup, one of the perks of needing to be around twenty-four seven sometimes. I don't have to share a shower with any of the other guys."

"Nice." I pointed at the small fridge, sink, and stovetop. "You even have a kitchenette."

He patted his abs. "Gotta have fuel nearby to keep me going."

"Makes sense."

He strode over to the closet and grabbed a big T-shirt that he handed to me. "My club business shouldn't take too long. Go ahead and get ready for bed. You can wear this."

"Bed?" I echoed, my brows drawing together. "It's only eight."

"You had a big day, baby. I bet you're more tired than you realize."

Thinking about the high of having my first date with him and the low of finding that note in the flowers on my doorstep, I had to agree. "You're probably right."

"I usually am," he murmured before giving me a quick kiss and walking out the door, locking it behind him.

7

WIZARD

Finally—*finally*—I had Thea right where I wanted her. With me.

Leaving her in my room was hard as fuck, but I needed to bring King up to speed and make sure he was on board with everything. As the president, he had every right to deny having Thea stay here and demand that I turn the investigation over to the police.

However, King was all about family and always had our backs, so I knew he would not only agree but also offer to help. Still, it was out of respect that I made the request.

When I walked into the lounge, King and his old lady were sitting on the couch, playing with their newborn son, Cadell.

His head came up as I entered, and his expression went from soft to his natural scowl. "Gotta handle some club shit, baby," he said to Stella. Then he pushed to his feet and turned, leading the way down another hallway to his office.

He knocked on Blaze's open door as we passed by, and the VP stood to follow us. Echo, Kevlar, Ace, and Ash were all with him, and he motioned for them to come with us.

King stalked into his office and over to his desk, dropping into the large leather chair behind it.

Blaze went to stand next to him, casually leaning back against the wall while Ash and Ace sat on the couch opposite the conference table, where Echo, Kevlar, and I took a seat.

"Wizard?" King muttered, giving me the floor.

I glanced at Echo. "You tell 'em anything?" I didn't want to waste time repeating anything he might have already shared, but he shook his head.

Quickly, I filled them in on the basics of Thea's situation. Then I looked at King. "She's good here?"

He nodded and waved off my question. "Of course. There's nowhere safer, and we protect our own."

I wasn't surprised that he'd picked up on what Thea meant to me, but I was grateful because I wasn't ready to talk about it with anyone until she and I were on more solid ground.

"You have the letters?" Ash asked, his fingers tapping on the table restlessly.

Nodding, I dropped the envelope on the table and slid it over to him.

"I'll have my contact at the private lab to see if there are any prints to analyze."

"Thanks," I grunted. "I haven't had a chance to do any more digging other than the flower shops, but I'll give you all any information as I find it."

"Ace, try to follow the money from the flower orders," King instructed.

It would be hard as fuck if they were all paid in cash, but Ace had done it before, so I was hoping he could get something for me now.

"Wizard, make sure you go over every detail with Thea. What's changed in her life? Especially around the time the stalking started," Blaze added.

Word would make it around to all of the club brothers shortly, and anyone available would help out however they could.

Family meant something different to the Hounds of Hellfire. It was a choice, not a genetic assignment. We were a solid wall of protection, respect, and honor. If you fucked with one Hound, you fucked with us all.

When King dismissed the meeting, I decided to go check on Thea before heading to my office to get to work. I should've known better.

The bathroom door was shut when I walked into the room, and I heard the sound of running water.

Shit.

Thea had obviously decided to take a shower, and now, all I could think about was her wet, naked body just on the other side of that wall. I wanted to see just how much wetter she would get with my fingers, tongue, or cock in her tight little pussy.

My dick was trying to punch its way through my zipper, and I winced when I turned to shut and lock the door.

Stiffly, I moved toward my dresser, intending to get changed before Thea emerged from the bathroom. My plan to work had gone out the window. I wanted to go to bed with her, even if all I did was hold her.

I kicked off my shoes and yanked off my socks, then my T-shirt, and tossed the clothes into the hamper. Carefully, I lowered my zipper and was about to pull myself out when I heard Thea's voice. Smiling when I saw her cell on the bedside table, I realized she was talking to herself. *Fuck, she was cute.*

I padded across the carpet to the door and listened.

"High Triangle? That definitely goes on the list."

"The Wheelbarrow? It's got potential."

"What about The Plunge? I think she'd be into it."

"Doggy style? Hmmm...no."

If I'd been moving, I would have frozen right then. *Wait. What?*

"The Erotic V? I think she could get on board with that...or on the table."

She giggled, and I shook my head, wondering if I was hearing this right.

"Rock and Ride? Probably not the first time."

Is she making a list of sex positions?

"Sexy Seesaw? Is it too much like Rock and Ride?"

"Sixty-nine? Nah, too early. Maybe when they've been together longer. I wonder if their height difference will make it more difficult?"

Holy shit. That's exactly what she's doing.

"Basic Missionary? Probably, but I can be a little more creative than that, right? Then again, don't knock it until you've tried it."

"Reverse Cowgirl? Doesn't seem like a position she would like—her loss, I would imagine."

Her comments after the last two surprised me. Didn't she start with the basics before getting creative? I shut off that line of thinking real fucking fast. The thought of Thea with another man made me feel like hunting each one down and putting a bullet between their eyes.

"I've got it!" she shrieked. "Against the wall in the shower! Of course, he'd have to be huge and strong like Baylor. He could definitely lift me and have his way with me—"

That shredded the last of my control.

Fuck it.

I opened the door and slipped inside, shutting it softly behind me. The shower was all glass on two sides, but it was foggy, so I could only see Thea's outline. Damn, she had more curves than I realized when she was clothed.

A hiss escaped my lips when I released my dick, the aching member popping up and slapping against my stomach.

Once I was naked, I stepped over to the shower and smoothly opened the glass door before stepping inside. Thea shivered, clearly feeling the small blast of cool air. But before she could turn and look, I stood behind her and cupped her hips, dragging her back against me.

She gasped when she felt my long, fat cock between us. My hands glided up her waist and rib cage until they were resting just under her tits.

"Sounds like you need to do a little research, baby."

"R-research?" she stuttered.

"You definitely need to try out some of the positions on the list you were making."

Thea's head dropped forward, and she sighed. "You heard that?"

I grinned and moved all of her hair to one shoulder so I could place a kiss on the exposed one as I put my hand back under her breast. My thumbs skimmed over the sensitive flesh as I answered with a chuckle. "You weren't being real quiet, baby."

Slowly, my hands crawled upward. "I want to know just how loud you can be," I murmured as I covered her tits with my big palms. "Perfect fit," I groaned.

Gently, I massaged the soft, round globes, and my cock twitched as her breathing became more erratic.

"Want to know what I was thinking even before

I heard you talking about me fucking you against the shower wall?"

I plucked her nipples, and she cried out, "Yes!"

One of my hands traveled south until I was cupping her pussy. "Knowing you were naked and wet from the shower, I wondered how much wetter I could make you." I plunged my middle finger into her channel, making her cry out. "Damn," I grunted. "You're tight as fuck."

Thea moaned, and a shiver wracked her body when I moved my digit in and out twice. "Wanna find out, baby?"

"Please," she begged, closing her thighs as if to keep me from withdrawing my hand.

I worked her with my finger, eventually managing to squeeze a second one in there until she felt slick with more than water. Then I withdrew them, and she whimpered. "Relax, baby. Gonna give you what you need. I just want to taste your juicy pussy."

I flipped her around and backed her against the wall, then dropped to my knees. "Gorgeous," I breathed as I got my first look at her bare pink pussy. Sitting back on my heels, I lifted one of her legs and put it over my shoulder, then leaned in and covered her center with my mouth. *Fucking hell.* She was soaked with a sweetness that was all her own.

Groaning, I cupped her ass to keep her in place as I devoured her sex. My cock was leaking steadily, swelling even more as I swallowed her nectar.

"Baylor," Thea moaned. Her fingers tunneled into my hair, and her pelvis undulated, seeking pleasure and relief.

Tearing my lips away, I ordered, "Louder, baby." Then I went back to feasting.

"Oh, yes. Yes! Oh, Baylor! Yes!"

As she neared climax, she shouted in ecstasy, but I still wanted more. I plunged a finger inside her and curled it up to rub her more sensitive area while I sucked hard on her clit.

I hummed in satisfaction when she screamed my name as she fell over the edge.

"Better than I imagined," I rasped as I placed a kiss on her mound and stood. Looking down at her hazy eyes and flushed cheeks made me want to do it all over again. And I would, eventually.

Instead, I bent my head and captured her lips in a deep, wet kiss, letting her taste her own sweetness on my tongue. My hands explored her body as we kissed, but then I ripped my mouth away as I cupped her ass and hoisted her up so her back was pressed against the wall. "I believe you were wondering about whether I could hold you up and fuck you while holding you up," I teased as her legs wrapped around my waist. "Since you're light as a fucking feather, I'd say it's looking pretty damn good."

I rubbed her center up and down against my dick a few times, then shifted her so that the tip of my cock was kissing the puffy folds of her pussy.

"Wait," she panted.

"Are you okay?" I asked, worried that I was hurting her in some way.

"Definitely." She sighed, then quickly continued, "I just...I think I should be honest about something before you go through with this."

My brow furrowed, and my mouth curved into a frown. "Have you lied to me about something, Thea?"

"Oh no! I meant that I hadn't told you everything. We haven't known each other that long and—"

"Baby," I groaned, pressing my forehead to hers and closing my eyes. "I'm holding on to my control by a very thin, frayed string, so I need you to hurry up."

Thea giggled, but it was more of a nervous sound than an amused one. "It's just...I know it probably seems like I have a ton of experience at sex and am writing from my own perspective, and—anyway, it's just that—um—"

"Thea!" I growled.

"I'm a virgin!" she squeaked.

I froze, thunderstruck at her announcement. Then I muttered, "Shit."

Thea whimpered and started struggling, trying to get out of my hold.

Yeah, that hadn't sounded how I meant it.

"Baby, just hold on a second. Let me explain. Baby! Thea!" I roared her name, and she finally quit wiggling. "Let me fucking explain, okay?"

She nodded, and I heard a little sniff that just about broke my heart. "If you don't want to do this—"

"Make no mistake, Thea," I interrupted in a steely voice. "I *will* fuck you tonight. You being a virgin won't stop me from making you mine. In fact, I'm ecstatic that you will be mine and only mine. The only thing it changes is *how* we fuck."

Her eyes lifted to meet mine, filled with confusion.

I sighed. "I can't be rough with you now. Since it's your first time, it's already going to hurt, and I hate that. I want to make it as painless as possible, and that requires control and tenderness. The reason

I swore was simply because I'm so fucking desperate to be inside you, I didn't have a clue how I was going to calm the hell down so I can make this good for you."

She sniffed again, and I wanted to punch myself for making her cry. "Really?"

"Really, baby. I want you so damn much that I can barely think straight. But one thing is for certain, I'm not gonna take you against the wall in the shower." I kept her wrapped around me as I took a step back and shut off the water.

Her expression fell, and I couldn't help chuckling, which annoyed her.

"This time, Thea. Not against the wall *this* time." I stepped out of the shower and reluctantly set her on her feet.

"Oh," she replied, her cheeks flaming with red. *So damn cute.*

"I promise, we'll fuck any way you want once you're broken in."

Her smile was a little shy when she giggled. "Promise?"

"Fuck, yeah, I promise!" I agreed enthusiastically, making her giggle again.

I grabbed a bath towel and quickly dried her off before doing the same to myself. Then I wrapped my hands around her waist and tossed her over my shoulder so I could open the door and hurry to the bed.

After dropping her onto the mattress, I quickly crawled over her, smiling as she continued to giggle. "First, I'm going to get your body primed," I informed her with a grin. "Then we're gonna try out that missionary position. See if you need more creativity."

Her blush deepened, and she placed her hands over her heated cheeks.

Lowering my body so I was covering her from head to toe, I bent my head and kissed her. Our lips slid against each other, and when I slipped my tongue into her mouth, she twisted and tangled hers with mine, doing an erotic dance that sent shock waves of bliss through me.

I was holding back through some kind of miracle, so I took advantage of it and spent as much time as I could—without losing my damn mind—getting her primed and ready for me. She was such a tiny thing, and I was practically a behemoth. Eventually, after three more orgasms and managing to work three fingers into her untried channel, I couldn't take any more.

"I need to fuck you," I said raggedly.

"Please, Baylor," she whimpered. "I can't wait any longer."

I pushed her knees up to her chest and then away from each other, opening her center as much as her body would allow. Then I leaned forward, bracing myself on my arms with my fists planted in the mattress on both sides of her.

When my cock was lined up with her hole, I slowly pushed inside. "Damn, baby. You're so tight. Fuck."

She whimpered, pain filling her eyes as my cock stretched her around its wide girth. I hadn't even breached her virginity yet. I dropped my head down and sucked one of her nipples into my mouth, gently biting and licking between deep pulls. I alternated between them as I slid one hand down her body until I reached the place where we were joined. Slowly, I used my thumb to rub circles around her little bundle of nerves. As her breathing picked up again, I moved the digit faster. When she was moaning loudly and writhing with desire, I punched my hips, popping her cherry and burying myself inside her from root to tip.

"Fuck!" I bellowed, my head thrown back as streaks of pleasure shot from my cock throughout my body.

I could barely catch my breath, but I finally opened my eyes and looked down at Thea in concern. "Are you okay?" I panted.

Keeping still was only going to last a little longer.

Thea inhaled and exhaled a few times, blinking back the tears glistening in her beautiful green eyes. It made my heart ache to know she was hurting, which made me feel guilty for the Neanderthal inside me yelling and banging on his chest that he'd claimed his woman. Thea was mine. All fucking mine.

"I think…I think it's okay now," she said softly.

Experimentally, I moved back a tiny bit before sliding back into place.

Her eyes grew wide and round, her lips forming a little o. "Wow," she whispered.

An arrogant grin spread across my face. "That's more like it."

Thea giggled, but it quickly became a moan when I pulled almost all the way out and thrust back in.

"Fuck," I grunted. "You're so tight, baby. Squeezing my cock like a damn vise. Fuck, yes!" Her inner muscles suddenly clamped down around me, practically making me see stars. "Oh, fuck!"

I shifted onto my knees and placed one of her

legs on each shoulder before palming her ass to lift her pelvis to just the right spot. My brain had deserted me, leaving me with nothing but the instinct to chase the ecstasy I knew was coming.

"Baylor!" Thea cried out. "Oh yes! Yes!"

"Play with those sexy tits," I growled.

She cupped her breasts and then twisted and plucked her nipples, gasping from the acute pain and pleasure.

"Good girl," I praised her, moving faster and pumping harder.

"Oh, oh! Yes! Yes! Yes!"

"Come, baby," I demanded, knowing I was seconds away from blowing my load. "Come now, Thea!"

I reached between us and pinched her clit, sending her soaring as she screamed my name.

Her pussy pulsed around my cock, and I suddenly remembered I was inside Thea without a condom. Before I could form even another thought in my mind, I roared as my dick exploded, shooting jet after jet of hot come into her unprotected womb. And the Neanderthal was once again beating his chest and hollering about breeding his woman.

The image of a naked Thea, with a big swollen belly, and in this exact position sent another wave through me, and I released even more of my seed inside her.

When I was empty, I collapsed down onto Thea, then rolled us over so I was on my back, staying buried inside her.

"There's no going back now," I murmured as I rubbed a slow circle on her back with one hand. "Then again, there was no going back before we even met. You were meant to be mine."

8

THEA

After the mind-blowing orgasms Baylor gave me, I felt like a boneless heap. One who could barely catch her breath. So I just sprawled against his chest while I waited for my pulse to stop racing and my lungs to start working properly again.

It took longer than I expected, which I made a mental note of for the next sex scene I wrote.

When I could finally speak again, I confessed, "That was even better than I ever imagined. And considering what I do for a living, I did a whole lot of imagining. A ridiculous amount really."

Stroking his palm down my bare spine, he murmured, "I know, baby."

He really did, which was so amazing. "I still can't

believe you've read all of my books. It's entirely possible that you're my biggest fan."

"I sure as fuck am the biggest in every way that counts."

He gently thrust up to emphasize his dick, which was still semi-hard even though he'd just come. Inside me, where he still was. Without anything between us—something we hadn't discussed yet. But also a topic I wasn't sure I wanted to bring up right now. Not until I had time to wrap my head around the fact that I wasn't bothered by him not using a condom even though I wasn't on birth control.

Even as my inner walls clenched around his hardness, I giggled. "I can't believe you said that. How old are you? Twelve?"

"Add twenty to that number, and you'd be right."

"You're thirty-two, huh?" I knew he was older than me, but I hadn't been sure by how much.

"Yup," he confirmed. "I have ten years on you, baby."

My eyes narrowed as I tilted my head back to glare at him. "How did you know that I'm twenty-two?"

"I know a fuck of a lot more than that." He shook his head with a deep chuckle. "Think about what I can do with a computer, Thea."

"Oh, right." Pressing my lips together, I sighed and rested my cheek against his pec again. "I guess that makes sense."

"I know my life isn't normal, baby. It means a fuck of a lot to me that you're willing to understand that."

I shrugged. "It's not as though mine is typical, either. A lot of people act weird when they find out that I write steamy romance, and you didn't judge me like others have done. It's only fair that I give you the same courtesy."

"I'm so damn lucky to have found you." He toyed with the ends of my hair, and each tug sent a sensual shiver down my spine. "Remind me to thank Echo."

"Because he brought Violet into your circle, and that's how you heard about me?"

"You could put it that way."

I poked his side. "Or you could just tell me what you actually meant."

"Because I looked into you a little when I did the background check on Violet that he asked for," he admitted.

"But why?" I asked. "I never even met her creepy neighbor."

"Your name came up since most of her narration

credits are books of yours, and I couldn't get it out of my head."

His perfect answer was yet another example of why he'd been so easily able to sweep me off my feet. Literally and figuratively. But I wasn't sure I was ready to do anything else sexual quite so soon again, so I focused on something that would hopefully cool my libido a little—work.

"Did you listen to some of her work for me?"

"Not once I realized there were sex scenes." He shuddered, his fingers digging into my butt cheeks. "Last thing I need is to hear Violet say shit like that. It did give me the perfect chance to give Echo some shit, though, about his woman narrating your sexy-as-fuck lines for the heroine while some dude did the hero's part."

"It isn't even like that," I chided with an exasperated huff. "Violet has only ever recorded her chapters for me separately from the male narrator. I was supposed to do a duet recording on my next stand-alone book, but I decided against it at the last minute."

"How come?"

I adored how genuinely interested he was in what I did. It was something I was looking for in a romantic partner, and he'd more than proved that he could deliver in this area. And more. "All of my other books are dual, and they do very well. The production company I use had talked me into giving duet a try, but I figured why fix something that isn't broken, you know?"

"I get the last part, but what the hell is the difference between dual and duet?"

I giggled at his grumpy tone. "In dual, the narrator does their entire chapter, giving voice to all of the characters in it. Which means that when Violet records for me, she delivers the files for her chapters without any interaction with the male narrator who does the hero's voice."

"Okay, that makes sense."

"But for a duet narration, she would give voice to the heroine whenever she speaks...including in the chapters that are in the hero's point of view," I further explained.

"Gotcha." His hold on me tightened. "Guess Echo's the one who owes you gratitude for canceling that project."

"Probably," I agreed, thinking about how possessive Echo was with my friend. Kind of like how the man holding me was with me. "Did you wonder what I'd be like in bed after reading my books?"

"Gotta tell you, I hadn't really thought about whether you'd tried the positions you wrote about."

I was stunned. All that worrying—and turning him down over and over again—had been totally unnecessary. "You didn't?"

"Not gonna pretend I didn't have a few pictures in my head when I read those scenes," he admitted. "The positions, kinky shit, and whatever can add to or take away pleasure. But it's not truly about how they're doing it that matters, baby. It's why they're doing it. On paper or in real life, the emotions behind the sex are what's important. And that's something you taught me."

I was afraid to ask exactly what he meant, but I was hoping he'd said that because he was falling for me the same way I was with him. "I guess this virgin had some sexy tricks up her sleeve after all."

"I heard you talking in the shower, so I know you do research, but I gotta admit that I'm blown away by the fact that you managed to write all those sex scenes without any experience yourself."

I trailed my fingers along the ridges of his six-pack with a grin. "I'm a very good researcher, no matter the topic."

"Like when you talked to my club brother about custom motorcycles?"

His voice had a slight edge to it, so I tilted my head back to peer at his face. Although we'd just had sex and he'd gotten absolute proof that I'd never been with anyone else, a muscle jumped in his jaw. It was almost impossible to believe, but I asked, "Are you jealous that I talked to Cross ages ago? On the phone? Without even giving him my name? Before we ever met?"

"Maybe a little."

His confession was so darn cute. And sexy.

"I never planned to tell you this..." I deliberately trailed off, waiting for him to demand that I finish my sentence.

I got exactly what I wanted when Baylor rolled me onto my back and levered his body over mine, the tip of his dick still notched inside me. His breath was hot against my mouth as he growled, "Tell me."

My cheeks heated as I wondered if my confession would be too much. "I...I—"

"Whatever you gotta say, you don't need to be afraid." He stroked his thumb across my bottom lip. "You can tell me anything, baby."

My voice was whisper soft as I admitted, "For the most part, my sex scenes have mostly been my own fantasies with a faceless guy. I figured if it was something that turned me on, then my readers would feel the authenticity."

"Makes sense," he grunted, a wrinkle popping up in the middle of his brow.

I smoothed it away as I continued to the part that was the most embarrassing, "But after I met you, the guy wasn't faceless anymore."

Heat flared in his dark eyes. "You tryin' to tell me that I'm the one you've been fantasizing about lately when you write sex scenes?"

"Yes."

"Fuck, baby." He claimed my mouth in a deep kiss that left me panting for more. "You can't say shit like that to me after I just popped your cherry."

"Who says so?"

"Me." He inched his now rock-hard dick a little deeper. "Don't want to hurt you, baby."

"Trust me, I'll be fine."

And I was...for three more orgasms before passing out.

9

WIZARD

I had dreamed about waking up with Thea in my bed for a month, but it was nothing compared to the real thing. Especially when her naked body was snuggled tightly up against mine.

She wiggled her cute little ass, turning my morning wood into a full-blown hard-on.

"You're playing with fire, baby," I rasped, my voice still gritty from sleep.

Thea giggled and shuffled around to face me. "I guess I'm just a thrill-seeking pyromaniac because those words just turn me on."

"You're gonna be the death of me, know that?" I groaned, burying my head between her head and neck.

"But what a way to go," she quipped.

I laughed and pulled back to look down into her sparkling green eyes. Despite her sassy words and tone, a blush was burning her cheeks. "Adorable."

She frowned. "Adorable is not exactly the description a woman wants to hear when she's naked in bed with a huge, sexy biker."

I kissed the tip of her nose. "It was a compliment, baby. Somehow, you manage to be adorable and sexy as fuck all at the same time."

"There you go again," she sighed, shaking her head. "Talking like my very own book boyfriend."

"Baby, don't you think that after writing book boyfriends for so many readers out there, you deserve a real one of your own?"

"Good grief," she muttered with a sniff. "You know how to make a girl swoon. Next thing we know, I'm going to be pregnant."

"That's the goal," I murmured.

Thea laughed, clearly not realizing I was being totally serious. "You Neanderthals are all the same. Hunt, steal, breed."

"Sounds like an excellent plan."

She tilted her head to the side and studied me as if to discern whether I was being hyperbolic.

"Come on, baby. We've both got shit to do. Let's shower and go get some food."

It took some coaxing to drag her out of bed, but I made it up to her by fulfilling my promise and fucking her up against the wall in the shower.

We found several of my brothers in the kitchen, chowing down on a breakfast casserole that smelled amazing. Courtney and Stella did a lot of the cooking these days, though most of us took the job here and there, so they had plenty of breaks. But many times, one of them would make breakfast or dinner and leave it for us to toss in the oven or even just eat cold. This casserole was one of our favorites.

"Gonna love this," I told Thea with a grin. "Courtney makes several at a time and freezes them for us to eat whenever we aren't in the mood to cook and neither of them are around."

As predicted, Thea loved the casserole, but as we walked out of the kitchen, I leaned down to whisper in her ear. "Still not as good as eating you for breakfast."

Thea flushed bright red, making me smirk wickedly, for which I earned a promise of retribution. "Bring it on, baby," I told her with a wink.

When we stopped at my office door, I unlocked it with a fingerprint and retinal scanner before ushering her inside.

"Wow," she breathed as she looked around the room. There was an entire wall of monitors, as well as several computers set up on the half-circle desk in the center of the room.

There was also a micro-kitchen installed on the wall next to the couch. King had it put in when I worked three days straight and forgot to eat. More than once.

A bunch of gadgets were also scattered around the room, ones I didn't explain the function of because they were top secret or illegal.

Once the little tour was done, I pointed at a desk, then the couch. "You can set up shop in either place. Wherever you're most comfortable."

Thea smiled and wandered over to the couch, flopping down on it, then wiggling around to get comfy.

Laughing, I handed her the laptop bag I'd been carrying for her, which had been tucked in her suitcase when I lugged her out of her house.

I pointed at a red button on the wall next to the door. "You need anything, press that."

"I thought you were never supposed to push the big red button," Thea said cheekily.

"It sends a signal to my headphones, playing a tone that lets me know someone is here or needs something." Rolling my eyes, I turned and walked around to sit at my desk. "And Blaze thought it was fucking hilarious to make it a big red fucking button."

"Okay," she replied, clearly repressing her laughter. "I'll try not to bother you."

"You're never a bother, baby," I stated. "I take care of what's mine. You need something, you come to me."

Thea huffed and crossed her arms over her chest, pouting. "That bossy, growly, possessive act should not be so hot," she snapped.

A grin spread across my face, and I winked at her as I put on my headphones. "But it is, so why keep fighting it?"

She glared at me, making me chuckle as I got down to business.

I compiled all of the information I had for Thea's stalker—which, admittedly, wasn't much. But I'd had less to go on before.

I set up several searches that would comb through every corner of the web that I could access. If they caught a whiff of something, it would alert me. Then I would dig deeper—usually that meant hacking a database or server.

After several hours, I hadn't made much

progress, although something about the flower delivery shops niggled at my brain.

I decided to analyze them more closely—their locations, clientele, employees, even their inventory. The first few times Thea received flowers, they'd all been different. Then somehow, the stalker discovered her favorite flower because from then on, it was always Gerbera daisies. Since they weren't sold at every shop, I ruled out those two. However, when I plotted them all out on a map, it felt like something was missing. So I added the discarded nurseries to the map, then stood back to look at it from a larger perspective.

As I scanned the map, a pattern popped out. The funny thing about random patterns is that they're never actually random. By attempting to make something appear random, you still end up with a pattern.

All of the stores were in different towns, but they weren't evenly spaced as most "random" patterns tended to be. There were clusters and sections where it looked like there should be a shop but wasn't. Some of that had to do with whether they sold the right plant.

The similarity that stuck out to me was the distance of all of them to one location. And when I took into account the dates the flowers were sent from each shop, it was clear that the stalker had started closer to this location and worked their way out to the shops an hour away but never went any farther.

The similarity point was a five-to-seven-mile grid about two towns over in the next county. I set up some bots to analyze specific data points about the area, then marked it out on a paper map.

Shortly after lunch, Ash sent me a text to head to Blaze's office.

"Need to get to a meeting, baby." I gathered up some of the information I'd collected, as well as one of my laptops. "You wanna stay here or go up to the room?"

Thea yawned and stretched her arms out. "I think I might go take a nap." She gave me an impish smile. "I didn't get much sleep last night." She shifted on the couch and winced. "And I'm a little sore."

I grinned, completely unrepentant. "I'll kiss it all better later," I promised as I fished a keychain out of my pocket. "This opens the door to our room. Make sure you get everything you need out of here. I'll get your biometrics in the system tomorrow so you won't have to wait for me to let you in."

Thea had been packing up her bag, but she

stopped to stare up at me. "You're going to put my finger and retina in your system so I can open the door without you here?"

"Yeah," I confirmed, puzzled at her reaction.

"How many other people can access this room without you?"

"King and Blaze."

"And now me."

"What's tripping you up about that, baby?"

"Well...it's just...in reality, we barely know each other."

My heated gaze scanned her from head to toe. "Beg to differ, baby."

Thea blushed hard and giggled. "The biblical sense doesn't count when it comes to trusting someone with access to everything you own. Particularly a fortune in equipment that I'm sure includes stuff I could be hauled away by the FBI, or whoever, just for knowing about."

"I can't give you access to the skiff room," I told her with a shrug.

"The what?"

"Skiff or S-C-I-F—a secure room or data center that protects sensitive security information from surveillance and leaks. Prez had it installed when he took over, and we started hiring out our...unique skills. It also doubles as a safe for other things we need to protect."

"Unique skills?" Her baffled expression reminded me that we hadn't discussed the workings of the club, particularly our main income source.

"Conversation for another day, baby. I need to get to my meeting."

"But you still haven't told me why you're giving me access to this room without you."

"Because you're mine."

Ash, Echo, and Ace were waiting with Blaze when I arrived, and I lifted my chin at them in greeting.

"King is on his way. From what he said and the sound of Stella laughing hysterically in the background, I gathered there was a diaper situation with Cadell." Blaze winced. "As in, I think it ended up all over him."

Echo guffawed loudly, and Blaze turned his gaze to the road captain and muttered, "Laugh it up, Echo. That's gonna be you soon enough."

That shut him up real fast since they'd just found out that Violet was pregnant a few days ago.

We talked about some other club business for a few minutes until King, Kevlar, and Cross strolled in.

Blaze's office was set up much like King's, but the conference table was a little smaller. We scattered around, sitting at the table, the couch, or other chairs in the room.

King looked at me, but I shook my head. "Might be onto something, but I want to know what Ash found first."

Ash sat across from me at the table, and he slid back the manila envelope he'd taken the day before. "Nothing," he stated grimly.

"Son of a bitch," I muttered. No prints left us with very little to go on.

King stood from the couch and moved over to sit next to me, then held out his hand for the envelope, which I passed along. He opened it and removed one of the letters, scanning it closely.

"I'll take a look at the ink," he offered. "There's a very slim chance that it could lead us to the printer that uses it. If I can figure out how old it is, and you can give us some kind of geographical lead, maybe we can match the printer to the buyer."

King had many talents, but his expertise was in forgery. He was also a former CIA agent. If anyone could pick up information out of ink and paper, it would be him.

I pulled out the map I'd drawn and spread it out on the table. "As a matter of fact, I think I can narrow down our search parameters to a town where the stalker either lives or works."

I explained my method for the findings, and we agreed that it made logical sense. It was at least a place to start.

"I'll get you a list of stores in that area who sell printers," I told King.

"This one is fast and on the higher end, but I still think it's a household printer and not larger office equipment."

I nodded and typed a few thoughts onto my computer notepad.

"You read all of the letters?" Blaze asked thoughtfully.

I shook my head. "Just got 'em from Thea yesterday and gave them straight to Ash."

"Why don't we go over them together and see if anything pops out at one of us?" he suggested.

It couldn't hurt, so I withdrew the stack of letters and began reading them aloud. Halfway through the first one, I recognized a specific sentence. I tapped on it and mused, "That's a line from *Monster Unmasked.*"

Instead of reading the rest aloud, I did it silently so I could get through them speedily. In each one, I stopped and pointed out at least one line, sometimes more.

"This is from *Snowbound.*

"This one is from *Sweetest Revenge.*

"This one from *The Monster Behind the Mask.*

"*Under the Blanket of Stars.*

"*The Spy's Return.*

"*The Darkest Hour.*"

On and on, line after line.

"Most of these lines are lifted directly from Thea's books. But they aren't ones you'd see in teasers, reviews, or any kind of marketing. This guy really knows these books."

"We sure the stalker isn't Wizard?" Echo said suddenly.

"The fuck?" I grunted, my head snapping up.

He shrugged, his face deadpan, but his eyes full of laughter. "You recognized all those lines, too. Either you know the books as well as the stalker, or it's you."

"Shut the fuck up, dickhead," I growled.

"Wasn't a denial," he crowed.

"I am not Thea's fucking stalker!"

"Maybe not," Ace conceded, "but you've clearly read her books."

"Research," I grunted. Then feeling guilty for being embarrassed, I added, "She's a fucking amazing writer. Don't care what genre it is. Until one of you reads a book Thea wrote, we're done talking about this."

Predictably, no one had a retort for that challenge.

"Keep working your angles," King said, changing the subject. "Anyone finds something, keep us all in the loop."

After a few more minutes of strategizing, everyone except Blaze, King, and me filed out.

"Something else on your mind, Wizard?" Blaze queried.

"Need a vest," I grunted. "With a property patch."

"Saw that coming," King drawled. "Lucky for you, the shipment of extra vests came in a couple of days ago."

"Also made a deal with a store in town that will get the names embroidered on there in twenty-four hours," Blaze added.

"Thanks." I nodded as I stood, then lifted my

chin at them in parting before I left to go find my woman.

10

THEA

My first two days at the Hounds of Hellfire compound were exciting—mostly because I lost my virginity and had way more sex than I expected so soon afterward. I assumed that the third would be pretty boring, but I was proved wrong late in the evening when one of the prospects brought another bouquet with a note for me. Not that I actually saw it because Wizard thrust his hand between us to grab the flowers before I could take them from the guy.

"What the fuck do you think you're doing?" he growled.

The prospect's eyes widened, and he gulped before answering. "Um...these flowers were dropped off for your woman, so I brought them in for her."

"You got one thing right...she's *my woman*," Baylor snarled. "If shit gets delivered here for her, it comes to me. Got it?"

The prospect nodded. "Yes, sir."

"Good, now get back to the gate."

The kid—who probably was about my age but seemed much younger—ran out the door of the clubhouse as though his pants were on fire.

"You didn't have to be so mean," I chided with a sigh.

"I sure as fuck did," Baylor disagreed, yanking the card from the flowers before striding to the bar to drop them into the garbage. "This is a safe place for you. Nothing is supposed to touch you while you're here."

I was about to point out that the prospect hadn't purposely done anything to hurt me, but I pressed my lips together when he started to read the note. My words dried up at the fury in his dark eyes, and I whispered, "How bad is it?"

"Worse than the last one," he grunted. "He's pissed that you're here with me. Doesn't get why you think you had to come to the club for protection when he'd never hurt you. He threw in some threats to me, which I expected. But the part that really pisses me off is that he might need to do something to you that he'll regret if you don't stay away from me when you're supposed to be his."

Baylor seemed angrier than I was scared, so I funneled my fear into soothing him. "But I'm not his. Can't ever be because I'm yours."

"Damn fucking straight you are," he growled, shoving the note into the inner pocket of his cut.

Interlacing our fingers, I urged, "So how about you take me to your room and remind me just how much I belong to you."

"That what you need right now?" he asked.

"It's what I want. Always," I confirmed, tugging him toward the hallway.

There was something extremely hot about how possessive he got, and I knew a way to reward him for looking out for me so well that I'd wanted to try since I first wrote it in a book.

"That fucker," he muttered, barely registering that I pulled him into his room and locked the door behind us.

He finally blinked, looking down at me. "We're going to find him before he has the chance to get close. You gotta know that, baby."

I nodded, taking his hands and pulling him toward the bed. "I know, but I don't want to think about him right now. I have something way better in mind."

He finally smiled, his whole body now standing at attention. "Oh?"

I sat down on the edge of the bed, pulling him between my legs.

Slowly, I shifted so I was on my back, turning around and scooting down until my head hung off the bed as I looked up at him. The anger drained from Baylor's gaze, quickly replaced by fierce desire.

"You sure this is what you want, baby?"

"Uh-huh. If my research was right, you'll be able to see your dick go down my throat as I taste you." Just saying the words had me on fire, and as soon as he pulled his pants down, revealing his dick, leaking at the tip, I couldn't help but lean up and lick the precome.

A deep groan rumbled up his chest. "Fuck, baby. I pictured you just like this when I read that scene."

I understood the mechanics involved with the position I wanted to try, but any nervousness I felt over trying something new paled in comparison to the excitement I felt over turning him on.

Leaning forward, Baylor placed his arms on either side of my hips as he slowly inched his cock between my lips. He didn't move fast, letting me take the lead as I sucked in the head, using my hand to stroke his shaft so that I didn't end up with too much in my mouth all at once. Just like the blow job scene I wrote.

"Yes, baby. You're such a good girl when you suck me just like that," he praised as his hands went to my leggings, pushing them down along with my panties until his fingers slid inside my wet center.

I got even more turned on that he'd taken my hint and was playing with me while I sucked his dick. I moaned around his shaft, my tongue licking the underside.

"You're enjoying this as much as me, aren't you?" he asked, thrusting his fingers in and out of me in rhythm with the movement of his hips as he fucked my mouth.

He was too deep for me to answer, to the point where I was almost gagging on his dick as it hit the back of my throat.

Then he pressed his thumb to my clit, and I moaned, bucking to meet his fingers.

"That's it, baby, come all over my hand. Show me that you're mine with my dick in your mouth and my fingers in your tight pussy."

As if his words pulled the orgasm from me, my

legs tightened around him, my whole body shaking as I came harder than I ever had before.

"Fuck yeah," he growled, leaning forward so his face was between my legs. Then he spread my legs so he could lick up every bit of my arousal dripping down my inner thighs.

I felt an aftershock with each swipe of his tongue, but that didn't stop me from swirling mine around the tip of his dick while it was still in my face. Too soon, he picked me up and flipped me around so that he was lined up with my entrance.

Wrapping my legs around his hips, he rasped, "Your mouth felt too damn good. If you keep going at my cock like that, I'm going to come, and that's reserved for your pretty little pussy."

We still hadn't had the actual conversation about continued lack of birth control, but I figured we both knew the risks we were taking. And judging by some of the stuff that he said about knocking me up when he was deep inside me, Baylor wasn't scared about possibly getting me pregnant. More likely, he was excited about it maybe happening. And so was I.

At some point, we'd have to talk about it—preferably before I was already pregnant. But not when he was about to sink his perfect dick inside me.

Then he filled me to the hilt with one powerful thrust, giving me exactly what I needed, and all of my thoughts scattered.

"This tight little pussy is mine and only mine. Isn't it, baby?"

"Yes," I gasped as he swiveled his hips, hitting a spot that I felt deep in my womb.

"Tell me," he demanded.

"I'm yours."

"Mine," he grunted, slamming into me. Hard.

It felt so good, and I was already close to another orgasm. My eyes drifted shut, but Baylor wasn't having it. "Eyes on me," he demanded. "And tell me again who this pussy belongs to while you fly apart for me. Let me see those gorgeous eyes of yours get all hazy while I make this pussy come for me, like it was made to do."

"I'm yours," I panted.

"Louder, baby. Tell me what else is mine." The pace of his thrusts sped up, and he slid his hand between us, circling my aching clit with his thumb as he pounded into me.

"My pussy is yours. All yours."

"Damn straight, it is. Now come for me. I want to feel you around my cock as I fill you. Everyone will finally know you're mine when you're carrying my baby in your rounded belly."

He proved yet again that I had a hidden breeding kink because his words sent me flying over the edge. I came hard, my toes curling and my entire body shuddering underneath him. After a few more pumps of his hips, I felt the warm splash of his come against my inner walls. Then his body collapsed on mine, although he was careful not to give me too much of his weight.

Rolling onto his side, he laid his head in the crook of my neck and peppered kisses there. I could barely move, my head lolling against the sheets.

We stayed connected for a few more moments before Baylor slipped out of me, and I whimpered, already missing the feeling of him.

"I love how much you hate to lose me after sex."

"Because your dick is mine, just like my pussy is yours," I rationalized with a grin.

"True." He kissed my temple before heading to the bathroom, giving me a perfect view of his naked butt. He returned shortly with a damp washcloth, cleaning between my legs before tossing it to the side.

"Cuddle me to sleep?" I asked, my eyelids growing heavy.

He laughed before sliding in next to me, his arms going around me so I could snuggle in against his warm chest. "Anything for you, baby."

11

WIZARD

Thea and I had both been worn out by the time I was done with her last night. We fell into an exhausted sleep, but it didn't last long for me. My eyes popped open when the sun was breaking over the horizon. The events of the day before flooded my mind and burned in my gut all over again.

I laid there for a bit, just holding my woman and reveling in the feel of her gentle curves pressed against my body.

But eventually, my mind was too restless to stay in bed. I carefully shifted Thea off me and quietly grabbed clothes before I went into the bathroom to shower. When I emerged, she was still fast asleep, so I left her a note, directing her to find me in my office.

I made a pit stop in the kitchen for a bagel, then got settled in front of my army of technology.

King hadn't had any luck pinpointing the ink and printer yet, so the only thing I could think of was to scan footage from security cameras all over the town where I was confident the stalker either lived or worked. Or both.

I also had a program going through all the footage from the cameras that had an angle on any of the flower shops. Mainly, I was hoping to find a familiar face at multiple places like the flower shops, a post office, the library, bookstores, etc.

With the delivery yesterday, I had a little something new to work with. The nursery he'd used was only a few minutes from the center of the town I was fixated on. I added the camera footage in and around the shop to my program. Then I went through it manually as I'd done with the other shops. Sometimes, the human eye caught things a computer dismissed and vice versa. I wasn't taking any chances with Thea's life.

At two o'clock, a man rode a Vespa into the store's parking lot.

A Vespa? What kind of grown man rides a fucking scooter?

But something was familiar about the vehicle. It

was silver and had every standard feature that all Vespas left the factory with. It was completely unmemorable.

Maybe that was what made it stick out to me. I didn't know a single person who hadn't customized their cars before or after they came off the lot. Motorcycles, bikes, scooters, skateboards...basically anything you could travel on. Even if it was something as simple as a single enhanced feature.

However, when I pulled up the specs for the most basic Vespa, it matched this one to a T.

I paused the footage and quickly pushed my chair in front of another computer and added the information for the scooter into my program.

Suddenly, it started spitting information at me. Not only was the Vespa on cameras at each of the flower shops but it was also seen all over town. Unfortunately, the license plate was obscured just enough to keep a camera from seeing it clearly but not so much that you'd get pulled over.

While the program continued to search for a common person near or on the vehicle, I went back to the footage from the most recent shop. The rider appeared to be a man with brown hair and a somewhat muscular build, of average height and with no distinguishable marks from the back. He kept his head down and turned away from the camera, as though he'd studied the location to find the best way to avoid them.

He went inside and came back out twenty minutes later. To my irritation, he had no overtly distinguishable marks from the front either. Even his clothes were plain and unremarkable.

I sighed and rubbed my eyes, tired from lack of sleep and frustration. When I focused back on the screen, the man's head was just turning down as if he'd looked up for a split second.

Did we finally catch a fucking break?

Putting the video in reverse, I let it play at a speed slower than a snail's pace.

A few frames later, I froze the screen, staring straight into the face of the man who I was certain had to be Thea's stalker.

Thirty minutes later, I had a full dossier on Mark Johnson—a.k.a. Mark Xavier, his stage name as an audiobook narrator who'd recorded a good portion of Thea's books. Including an FBI file. Turned out, he'd applied for the bureau but hadn't passed the psych eval.

He also had a sealed juvie record. Or the file *was* sealed until I got ahold of it. And several undisclosed settlements for cases where charges had been brought up on him for voyeurism, stalking, breaking a restraining order, and similar.

No wonder he chose to make his living as a narrator. He didn't need to interact with almost anyone in person.

It was just after nine, so I sent a text to King, then printed several copies of an abridged dossier. He replied to meet in his office in half an hour. Both King and Blaze had homes built on the compound, so they were able to get to the clubhouse for a meeting in minutes. However, while a lot of the patches lived on-site, plenty of them had their own homes and would take a little longer. Echo and Violet would live the farthest away once they moved into their house. Still, it was less than twenty minutes, but getting out the door took them a while, so King's set time allowed all the key players in this operation to get here. Two minutes before our scheduled meeting, I gathered up the files and my computer, then headed to the prez's office.

King, Blaze, Echo, and Kevlar were already there when I arrived. Ash and Ace owned homes a few minutes away, but Ash walked in less than a minute after me, and Ace was hot on his heels.

When everyone was seated around the conference table, I passed a folder to each person. "Got an

ID," I announced. I waited while they scanned the information and predictably, I heard several curses.

"How is this motherfucker still roaming free?" Kevlar barked.

King leaned back in his chair and shoved the file away. "He won't be for long."

There were several murmured agreements, and satisfaction roared through me. I'd been confident that my brothers would be on my side about this pathetic asshole, but I'd needed to hear the confirmation.

My cell vibrated in my pocket, and I checked my watch to see that Thea had texted me.

> **THEA**
>
> Good morning! I'm headed downstairs. Should I still meet you in your office?
>
> **ME**
>
> Good morning, baby. Sorry, but I ended up in a meeting. If you want to wait in my office, I should be less than an hour.
>
> **THEA**
>
> Sure! I'll get some writing done. I have all kinds of new inspirations…

I laughed and waved off everyone's curious looks.

> ME
>
> Happy to be of service anytime.

She sent back a laughing emoji, then one blowing a kiss.

So fucking cute.

Her mention of the night before reminded me that I'd been fucking her bare, and while it was unlikely, she could already be knocked up. I'd noticed that she could go down a rabbit hole like I did when I was working and often forgot to eat.

> ME
>
> Stop in the kitchen and eat some breakfast.

> THEA
>
> Well, aren't you bossy this morning?

I grinned as I typed my response.

> ME
>
> You like it when I'm bossy, growly, and possessive.

Three dots jumped on the screen, then disappeared, and showed up again before a text came through.

> **THEA**
> I'm trying to come up with an argument. Hold please.

This time, I couldn't contain my huge burst of laughter. Even in the shitty situation we were in, she brought light into my life.

> **ME**
> Doesn't matter. I'll prove it to you later.

> **THEA**
> Promises, promises.

I sent a winky face—something I was sure I'd never done before in my life—before tucking my phone back into my pocket.

"We have your attention again?" Blaze asked.

"If that had been Courtney?"

Blaze shrugged. "Touché."

We spent the next hour running through possible scenarios, then settled on two and decided to put both balls in motion to see which one moved along the fastest.

12

THEA

Entering Baylor's high-tech office without him felt weird...but also awesome because it was a sure sign of how much he trusted me. Being surrounded by his scent got me into the zone much more quickly than usual. So much so that I wasn't sure how long he'd been watching me when I finally looked up from the scene I just finished writing. "Okay, creeper."

"Not my fault you still haven't worked on your situational awareness."

"Ugh, that's fair," I groaned, stretching my arms above my head. "Especially when I'm lost in a fictional world."

He set his computer on the desk. "Book going well?"

"It really was." I beamed a smile at him. "I know I joked about the inspiration you gave me, but you just might be my good luck charm. I've never gotten so many words in such little time. And I'm even in love with what I've written so far instead of doubting every letter I type."

"Happy for you, baby."

He strode toward me and leaned down to kiss me, leaving me wanting more. But before I could ask for another, I spotted the face of his watch. "Oh no. Is that the time? Crap."

His brows drew together. "Why does it matter what time it is?"

"Because I totally forgot that I have a meeting with my audiobook production company today. Luckily, I set a reminder for two hours prior on my calendar, which pinged about ninety minutes ago." I nudged him out of my way so that I could stand. Shoving my stuff into my laptop bag, I added, "The reason that I went with them is because they're actually local, which is pretty unusual. But it's been awesome because meeting with them forces me away from the computer and into the real world sometimes. And it's how I met Violet."

"Who're you meeting with there?" he asked,

following me closely as I left the office to go to his room and change.

"Susan, she's the owner of the production company." I ducked into his closet to find something more presentable to wear. Not that I needed to dress up, but Baylor's oversized shirt and a pair of leggings wouldn't work. And it was too warm to just toss a sweatshirt over it, so I swapped out shirts for one of my own before heading into the bathroom to brush my teeth.

When I finished, Baylor was shoving his feet into his boots. At my look of confusion, he explained, "I'm comin' with you."

I hadn't left the compound since he brought me here after learning about my stalker. In my rush to get to the meeting, I hadn't stopped to think about how this would all work. "Thank you."

"Already told you that you don't need to thank me when I do shit for you," he growled.

"I know, but that doesn't mean I'm not grateful." I beamed a smile at him. "Or that I'm not coming up with all sorts of creative ways to demonstrate it."

"Fucking hell, woman," he groaned, reaching down to adjust the bulge in his jeans. "It's a damn good thing we're taking my truck because driving my bike with a hard-on wouldn't be fun."

After slipping my shoes onto my feet, I winked at him. "We'll save that for another time when we can make it all sorts of fun."

He shook his head with a deep chuckle. "Have I mentioned lately how fucking lucky I am that you're mine?"

"You may have mentioned it a time or two." And I had swooned whenever he did, falling more in love with him.

"Good, because you deserve to hear it."

"Later," I urged, practically pushing him out the door. "Right now, we need to get going so I'm not late."

Baylor didn't waste any time getting us to his truck, but that didn't stop him from calling out to a couple of his brothers on the way through the clubhouse. We ended up with Ash and Kevlar trailing behind us on their bikes.

"Don't you think this is a little bit of overkill?" I asked when we parked in front of the production company's office. "I didn't even remember I had this meeting, so there's no way my stalker could've known."

"Not gonna take any risks when it comes to your safety, baby," he growled.

"We got your backs," Ash confirmed as he got off his motorcycle.

Kevlar nodded. "Yup."

At first, I felt a little weird walking into the meeting with three bikers, but then I decided to just own it. I wrote steamy romance novels, and Susan's company handled the recording of them. A few hot guys listening in shouldn't distract us from discussing business. Not that I really noticed Ash or Kevlar when I only had eyes for Baylor.

The same couldn't be said for the receptionist, whose gaze darted between all three men while she tripped over her words. Luckily, Susan came to her rescue and ushered us into the conference room without blinking an eye over my unplanned entourage.

When I spotted Mark waiting at the table, I realized she had a surprise for me of her own. Swiveling my head toward her, I asked, "Why is he here?"

Her reply about wanting to revisit the topic of duet narration was drowned out by Mark's roar. "The better question is why the fuck is that fucking biker here?"

Everything happened so quickly. I wasn't sure how he got out of his seat and over to me so fast, but before I knew it, Mark was holding a knife to my throat.

Baylor shoved Susan out of the way and demanded, "Let her go, Johnson."

"So you're not as dumb as you look," Mark snarled. "I didn't think you'd figure out who I was before I made Thea understand how badly she was fucking up, messing around with you when she's mine."

It was a good thing Ash and Kevlar had followed us because they barely managed to restrain Baylor when Mark tried to claim me.

"Calm down, man. You gotta get your head straight so we can save your woman," Kevlar urged, gripping his right shoulder while Ash held the left.

"Fuck," Baylor groaned, a muscle jumping in his jaw.

"She's not his woman," Mark screamed. "Thea just went with him because she was confused by my notes. If she'd realized they were from me, she never would've gone on a fucking date with him for burgers in the first place, let alone let him talk her into staying at your dirty biker compound."

I really wished I'd taken Baylor's warnings about my lack of situational awareness to heart much sooner. Maybe then I would've realized that my favorite male narrator was also my stalker.

"If you saw us together, then you gotta know she's not yours," Baylor pointed out, his gaze locked on my terrified one.

The confidence in his dark eyes helped ease some of the tension in my body. At least as much as it could when there was a knife pointed at my throat. The downside to all of the research I had done for books over the years was that I knew how close that sharp tip was to my jugular vein. One wrong move, and I would bleed out too quickly for Baylor to save me.

"You're wrong," Mark yelled, tightening his hold on my arm.

"Mark, please. You're hurting me," I pleaded.

"I'm sorry, sweetheart, but sometimes we have to use tough love to help the people who are most important to us."

There wasn't an ounce of apology in his tone, just anger. I wasn't sure how I was going to get out of this. Not until Baylor mouthed, *"The Spy's Return."*

Reading my books hadn't just convinced me to go out on a date with him, it also allowed us to speak in code with each other. All it took was the title of that particular book for me to understand what he was getting at.

After taking a deep breath, I let my body relax so I wasn't struggling against Mark's hold. Then I whispered, "You're right."

"C'mon, Thea. You can't listen to this guy," Baylor argued. "He has a knife to your fucking throat."

"Shut the fuck up," Mark screamed. "You're the one she shouldn't listen to because you're just confusing her."

"Stop, Wizard." I deliberately used his road name in the hope that the other guys—who'd only ever heard me call him Baylor—would understand that I was just playing along. "You need to leave."

"Leave?" he echoed, clenching his fists at his sides as he shrugged Ash's and Kevlar's hands away from his shoulders. "Just walk away and let this guy hurt you?"

"Mark won't hurt me. He loves me."

"I do," Mark whispered, his hold on me loosening.

The knife moved about half an inch away from my throat, giving Baylor just enough space to lunge forward and rip me away from Mark. Then he was on him, clenching his wrist so hard that the knife fell to the floor with a dull thud. After kicking it out of the way, Baylor punched Mark in the face. Blood spurted from his nose, but that didn't stop Baylor from hitting him again. And again. And again.

Ash held me while Kevlar rushed forward to pull Baylor off him. "It's done. I got him. He's not gonna hurt your woman ever again."

"I don't understand," Susan whispered. "What just happened?"

"You invited my stalker to our meeting."

13

WIZARD

I spun around, and as soon as I spotted Thea, I opened my arms. She ran at me full speed, nearly knocking us both to the ground when her body collided with mine.

"You okay, baby?" I asked, holding her tightly against me.

"I am now," she said softly.

When I realized she was trying not to cry, my arms tightened around her. "That was a fucked-up situation. Not gonna think less of you for crying."

"It's so stupid," she grumbled, then sniffed and buried her face against my chest.

"Just makes you my damsel in distress," I teased. "And playing the hero is good for my ego."

Thea giggled, and I kissed the crown of her head before scooping her into my arms.

"Hey," Ash said as he walked up beside us. "Nice move, Thea. How'd you know what Wizard was planning?"

She looked at him with a grin. "He mentioned *The Spy's Return*."

At Ash's puzzled expression, she explained in more detail. "There's a scene where the heroine is confronted by the villain. He gets the drop on her, and when the hero shows up, the bad guy is holding a gun to her head.

"She plays along like he's the one saving her and drops her head back and to the side, ostensibly to look up at him. This moves the barrel so it's pointing just beyond her and exposes the villain's head just enough for the hero to take him out. So I relaxed and played along with Mark until Baylor had the perfect opportunity to save me."

Ash scratched his cheek and shook his head. "You got all that from the title of a book."

Thea twisted her neck to look up at my face. "We have our own kind of...shorthand," she mumbled with a sly smile.

"That kinda thing happens when you're in love," I drawled to Ash.

Thea gasped and stiffened. Silently, I shouted at myself for being a stupid motherfucker. This was not the time or place for her to hear me tell her that I loved her for the first time.

She stared at me with a stunned expression, and her mouth opened to say something.

I shook my head, then gave her a quick, hard kiss. "Not here."

Thea pursed her lips together before nodding.

"You got this?" I asked Ash.

He waved me off. "Yeah. We're good."

With a muttered, "Thanks," I rapidly exited the building. When we were settled in the truck and on our way home, Thea cleared her throat.

"Not yet," I told her gently, giving her thigh a pat before resting my hand there.

When we arrived at the clubhouse, I parked and got out of the vehicle. Thea obediently waited for me to jog around the hood of the truck and open her door.

"Good girl," I praised quietly, smiling when her cheeks turned pink and she shivered.

Then I engulfed her hand in my much bigger one and led her through the front door.

"Got one stop to make, then we'll go to our room and talk," I promised her.

Lucky for me, Blaze was in his office when we stopped by.

"That package arrive?" I asked in lieu of a greeting.

Blaze nodded and pointed at a box sitting on the conference table.

"Appreciate it," I muttered gratefully as I picked the package up and stuck it under my arm.

Thea looked at me expectantly, and I smiled, shaking my head. "Patience, baby."

She huffed and glared at me as I towed her to the stairs and up to our room.

Once inside, I ushered her to the little sitting area and gently pushed her down onto the couch before sitting on the coffee table right in front of her. It was a sturdy piece of furniture, and I knew it wouldn't break under my weight.

"That was a shit move," I told her softly. "Saying I loved you in the middle of the chaos like that."

Her head dropped forward, and she whispered, "It wasn't true?"

Scowling, I cupped her chin and forced her head up. "Didn't I promise never to lie to you?"

Thea chewed on her bottom lip, then conceded, "Yes."

"I love the fuck outta you, woman. Just meant that the timing was bullshit."

"Oh." Her lips lifted at the corners of her mouth, and her green eyes brightened. "You really love me?"

"Didn't I just say that?" I growled.

Her smile grew, and she beamed at me.

"Probably shoulda told you sooner," I admitted. "But with all the shit happening around us, it never seemed to be the right time."

"That makes sense," she agreed softly.

I waited a little bit, then raised an eyebrow and gave her chin a squeeze. "Got something to say to me, baby?"

Thea's cheeks turned pink, and she tried to duck her head but couldn't because I was still holding her chin.

"I thought maybe...um"—her eyes darted to the box sitting beside me on the coffee table—"I guess I was hoping you, um, had more to say?"

Laughing, I leaned in and gave her a quick kiss. "Patience, baby."

Her face screwed up in annoyance, making me chuckle again. "Tell me what I want to hear, and I'll give you your presents."

"Presents?" she repeated, perking right up. I'd

quickly learned that even though Thea didn't like to be snuck up on, she loved surprises. And presents.

"Tell me, baby," I insisted, making my tone extra gritty because I knew it turned her on.

"I love you," she said with a sweet smile and a dreamy sigh.

"Good girl." I released her chin, but not before taking another fast kiss.

She put out her hands and made a "gimmie" motion with her fingers.

"So greedy," I teased as I picked up the box and set it on her lap.

Thea's legs bounced with delight as she took off the lid. She stared at the contents, then tears well up in her eyes. It would have freaked me out if she hadn't also had a giant smile. "You want me to be your old lady?" she asked as she picked up the leather vest and admired the patch on the back.

"Fuck, yes," I grunted. "I want everyone who looks at you to know you belong to me."

Taking the vest from her, I stood and held it out so she could slip it on. Her fingers danced over her name, embroidered over her right breast.

"I love it," she whispered as her watery eyes met mine. "Thank you."

"One more thing," I mumbled before strolling to

the closet and reaching up to a shelf I knew was too high for her to access. "I want you to be mine in every way, Thea. The more ways people can see that you're taken, the better."

With the small velvet box clutched in my fist, I returned to sit in front of her.

"Got my vest on you, gonna put a baby in your sexy belly, and"—I opened the box to show her a sparking engagement ring—"you're gonna have my ring on your finger."

Thea giggled. "Is this your way of asking me to marry you, Baylor Chadwick?"

"No," I stated emphatically. When her eyes filled with confusion, I quickly cleared up the misunderstanding. "This is me telling you, we are getting married." I yanked her left hand forward and tenderly slid the diamond ring onto her fourth finger.

"Since you asked so nicely..." she teased.

I grabbed her hips and lifted her onto my lap, straddling me. "If you need a little convincing, I have plenty of ideas."

"I don't need convincing to marry you," she breathed, a shudder wracking her body when I palmed her ass and dragged her close so our chests and groins were stuck together.

"I meant convincing you to get married as fast as possible."

"Depends on your definition of fast," she told me suspiciously.

Grinning, I pushed to my feet and moved toward the bed. "We can agree on that after I've given you several orgasms."

Thea sighed. "Not fair. You're cheating using your caveman tactics and giant dick to make me agree to whatever you want."

"Would I do that?" I asked innocently, before tossing her on the bed.

"Yes," she panted a few hours later, her lips pursed in's sexy pout.

"I guess you're right," I acquiesced. "But I'm holding you to it, baby. You've got four weeks to plan a wedding." Grinning, I winked at her. "Besides, we wait much longer and you might not fit in your dress."

Thea gasped, and her hands immediately went to her stomach. "I didn't think of that!"

She jackknifed up in bed and quickly scooted away.

"Where the fuck do you think you're going, baby?" I growled.

"I have so much to do!" she cried as she put her

feet on the floor. Before she could stand, I curled my arm and around her waist and hauled her back onto the bed, then rolled her onto her back and covered her body with mine.

"Tomorrow," I stated before lowering my head to place a trail of kisses along her jaw.

"But—"

Four orgasms later, I'd convinced her to start planning our wedding tomorrow.

EPILOGUE
THEA

Baylor turned into a bit of a helicopter fiancé after everything that went down with Mark. I didn't blame him, though. Those five minutes had been the scariest of my life. And I loved how he wasn't afraid to show me just how much I meant to him in every way.

I rethought that a few minutes later when I got lightheaded on our way to the kitchen for breakfast, though. We'd been splitting our time between my rental house and his room here while we looked for a place big enough for us both.

As my vision darkened and I saw spots behind my eyelids, I wished this was one of the mornings when we were at my house instead. It would be a heck of a lot less embarrassing to faint in the privacy of my own home without any of his club brothers around.

"Fuck, baby. Are you okay?" Baylor rasped as his arms wrapped around me.

"Just a little lightheaded," I whispered, pressing trembling fingers over my eyes.

"Someone get Razor," he yelled.

I felt slightly better when he plopped me onto a barstool. "Asking for a doctor seems like overkill, even if he's one of your club brothers."

"You're pale as fuck and almost fainted. You need to be checked out by someone who knows what the hell they're doing."

I knew him well enough to assume he wouldn't back down, but I still complained, "Ugh, really?"

"Yes, really." Glaring over his shoulder, he demanded, "Call an ambulance."

I rolled my eyes as Ash stabbed his finger against the screen of his phone, not realizing until later why he was so quick to make the call.

It only took five minutes for the ambulance to arrive, and two paramedics rushed into the clubhouse. The guy asked what was going on, and while Baylor explained, the woman came over to me.

"You don't look so good. Is there any medical history I need to know about or pre-existing conditions?"

"Nope, I've always been as healthy as a horse."

"That's good to hear." She flashed me a quick smile before pulling a blood pressure cuff out of her bag. "I'm Nora. What's your name?"

"Thea."

"Enough chitchat," Baylor barked. "What's wrong with my woman?"

"Careful," Ash warned for some reason.

After Nora took my vitals, she asked, "Is there any chance you're pregnant?"

"A whole lot of them," I confirmed. "But only over the past two weeks, so isn't it too soon for me to be having symptoms like this?"

"Nope." She repacked her equipment into her bag. "Your blood pressure is normal. Same with your temperature and pulse ox."

The tension drained from my body as I started to hope that the reason I had been lightheaded was the best one possible. "That's good to hear."

"The dizziness passed fairly quickly, and it's often one of the first symptoms a woman experiences during pregnancy since it can be caused by hormonal changes or increased blood volume," she explained.

"My recommendation is that you have your man send his friend out for a pregnancy test and take it as soon as possible."

"His friend?" I asked, my brows drawing together.

"That one." She pointed at Ash. "It'll probably embarrass him, which would be awesome."

"Wouldn't be bothered by it at all, Nora," Ash disagreed.

She completely ignored him, her focus remaining on me. "If the test is positive, make an appointment with your gynecologist. If it's negative, go in to see your primary care physician, even if you don't get faint again. Better be safe than sorry."

Baylor squeezed my shoulder. "She'll see a doctor soon, either way."

"Good," Nora replied.

She'd done her best to ignore Ash, but I caught the soft look in her eyes when she glanced up at him earlier. She probably thought nobody was looking because everyone was paying attention to me, but she hadn't counted on me not staring at myself, which would've been weird.

"What was that all about?" I asked after she left with Ash hot on her heels.

Baylor laughed, shaking his head. "Ash managed

to piss Nora off when he got shot. Before he realized that she's the woman for him."

After having a knife shoved against my throat by my stalker, I barely blinked at the mention of one of the guys getting shot. "Sounds as though there's quite the story there."

"There definitely is." He pressed a kiss against my forehead. "But unfortunately for you, I can't share much of it because the whole thing was club business."

"That's probably for the best." I grinned up at him. "You should probably also warn all the guys... having an author in your life means that any stories I hear are fair game for books later on."

"Be prepared to take lots of notes, baby. My club brothers are a fucking riot when they're falling for their old ladies."

Considering what had happened with us, I believed him.

"Will do," I murmured as he gently lifted me off the stool.

He kept his arm around my back to make sure I was steady on my feet. "But wait until we get that pregnancy test to confirm you're carrying my baby."

Only twenty minutes later—with a whole lot of

hovering by Baylor—we had our answer. I was pregnant. Luckily, my wedding plans were already in full swing, so I didn't need to worry about not fitting into my dress.

EPILOGUE
WIZARD

My eyes drifted to the digital picture frame perched on my desk in my home office. When no one was in here with me, a single push of a button turned the screen into a camera feed. One that was set up in my wife's home office a few feet away.

I watched Thea for a few minutes, simply admiring how fucking beautiful she was. She'd gained a few more curves after having our daughter, Skye, four years ago, then our son, Wyatt, who just turned one. She'd complained only once because I spent several hours convincing her that she was the sexiest woman on the whole damn planet. I also made her tell me before I let her come—every single time.

Even though we were only separated by a wall, I liked being able to see her whenever I wanted. And it came in extremely handy in moments like this.

Her lips were curved in a little smile, her green eyes staring dreamily at her computer screen. Then she blushed and shifted restlessly in her seat.

I immediately shot to my feet. Those were her tells—signals that told me she was writing a steamy scene in one of her books.

Thankfully, Skye was at preschool, and Wyatt was having a playdate with Violet and Brendan.

After flipping the screen back to a montage of family photos, I padded out of my office and turned left, taking one step before I was at her door.

Wanting to catch her off guard, I didn't bother to knock. When I entered, she gasped and spun around in her chair. She looked even more flushed—all hot and bothered—in reality.

"Doing okay, baby?" I asked with a grin as I sauntered toward her. "Or am I just in time to help you find satisfaction from the scene in your book?"

Her eyes narrowed, but my grin widened when her breathing picked up, and her gaze briefly dropped to the bulge in my jeans.

"How do you always know when I'm writing a sex scene?" she demanded.

"A sixth sense?" I suggested, evading the truth without lying.

She pressed her lips together and shook her head. "I don't think so. It's happened too many times to be a coincidence."

I closed the distance between us, bending down to cage her in her chair with my hands gripping the armrests. "Prove it," I teased.

Suddenly, she gasped, and her eyes darted around the room. "Did you put cameras in here, Baylor?"

I tried to make my expression innocent but failed when a salacious grin spread across my face. "How else am I gonna know when my woman needs me?" Winking, I bent down until our lips were just inches apart. "Wouldn't want you to get stuck without inspiration. Or experience."

"Experience?" she questioned.

"That office romance you wrote last year was a bestseller," I reminded her smugly. "That scene in chapter twenty was real fucking familiar."

Thea blushed hard, and her green eyes turned molten with desire. "Ummm..."

"This the book about the computer nerd who falls for a chef and turns all possessive and growly?" I asked with a smirk.

"Yes," she whispered, her body leaning in closer. Her head dropped almost all the way back so we were looking at each other face-to-face.

She yelped in surprise when I scooped her into my arms and stalked out of the office. "What are you doing?"

"Giving you somethin' to write about, baby."

The kitchen was all kinds of dirty by the time she was screaming my name.

A month later, I walked into the bedroom to see Thea glaring at me with her hands propped on her hips.

I swallowed my amused smile. She was fucking adorable when she was pissed. Probably because she was so tiny. "Somethin' on your mind, baby?"

"Normally, I love that I have my very own book boyfriend and happily ever after, but this is getting out of hand," she snapped.

I raised an eyebrow and tilted my head, studying her. "Gonna need more explanation."

"These spontaneous sexcapades you initiate always seem to end up with me knocked up!" She threw her hands in the air and flopped down on the bed, lying on her back with her legs dangling over the side.

"You're pregnant?" I croaked, suddenly a little choked up.

"Yes," she grumbled. "This is the second time you've barged into my office and put a baby in me."

I padded across the room and leaned down, placing an arm on both sides of her. "You're not happy about the baby?" I asked even though that didn't seem like my Thea.

"Of course, I'm happy, you big lug!" she gasped, clearly offended that I'd insinuated otherwise.

"Then what's with the attitude, baby?"

"I wish we planned for me to get pregnant instead of you just stuffing me with sperm and leaving a little bun in my oven."

Grinning, I brushed my lips over hers, then whispered, "But it's so much fun making the dough."

Thea giggled and slid her arms around my torso, urging me down so she could wrap me in a tight hug. "True."

I captured her lips in a deep kiss while my hands splayed over her flat belly, then up to cup her tits.

"Mommy! Daddy! It's wunch time!"

Groaning, I dropped my head into the crook of Thea's neck while she giggled.

"Forgot the kids are home," I grumbled.

Thea patted my bicep. "We can celebrate after they are in bed tonight."

I winked and grinned wickedly. "We'll practice making more dough."

Thea's eyes went wide. "Just how many buns are you intending to put in my oven?"

I shrugged. "As many as you'll let me."

She sighed and pushed against my chest when Skye called out again, her voice closer to our bedroom now. "Let's talk about it next time."

I didn't say anything because I couldn't promise it wouldn't happen again.

Shortly after we had Madison, I realized it had been a good thing I hadn't committed to anything, or I would have accidentally lied to Thea.

When the pregnancy test came out positive, she huffed and muttered, "I'm going to start locking my office door when I'm writing sex."

That proved to be untrue since, after Chad, we made our next baby when I took her to a cabin to finish a book because she was up against a deadline.

I wouldn't take the blame for that one. She'd practically jumped me when I came inside after chopping wood.

"That's it," she panted after giving birth to

Mason. "That's the last of your giant babies I'm pushing out."

Honestly, as much as I loved seeing Thea round with our baby and wouldn't mind having more kids, I was tired of seeing her in so much pain during the birth. After five babies, I didn't want to put her through it anymore.

"Whatever you want, baby," I told her sincerely.

"But um..." Thea blushed, and I tilted my head, watching her with amused curiosity. "That doesn't mean the sexcapades have to end."

I laughed, then kissed her softly. "Of course not. Where would you find all of your inspiration?"

Want to find out how Ash manages to woo Nora? Find out in Ash!

And if you join our newsletter, you'll get a FREE copy of The Virgin's Guardian, which was banned on Amazon.

ABOUT THE AUTHOR

The writing duo of Elle Christensen and Rochelle Paige team up under the Fiona Davenport pen name to bring you sexy, insta-love stories filled with alpha males. If you want a quick & dirty read with a guaranteed happily ever after, then give Fiona Davenport a try!

Printed in Great Britain
by Amazon